Some heroes wear capes. Some prefer sensory sacks.

Emmet Washington has never let the world define him, even though he, his boyfriend, Jeremey, and his friends aren't considered "real" adults because of their disabilities. When the State of Iowa restructures its mental health system and puts the independent living facility where they live in jeopardy, Emmet refuses to be forced into substandard, privatized corporate care. With the help of Jeremey and their friends, he starts a local grassroots organization and fights every step of the way.

In addition to navigating his boyfriend's increased depression and anxiety, Emmet has to make his autistic tics acceptable to politicians and donors, and he wonders if they're raising awareness or putting their disabilities on display. When their campaign attracts the attention of the opposition's powerful corporate lobbyist, Emmet relies on his skill with calculations and predictions and trusts he can save the day—for himself, his friends, and everyone with disabilities.

He only hopes there isn't a variable in his formula he's failed to foresee.

D1214965

Heidi Cullinan, POB 425, Ames, Iowa 50010
Copyright © 2017 by Heidi Cullinan
Print ISBN: 978-0-9961203-9-5
Print Edition
Edited by Sasha Knight
Cover by Kanaxa
Proofing by Lillie's Literary Services
Formatting by BB eBooks

First publication 2017
www.heidicullinan.com

SHELTER THE SEA

The Roosevelt, Book 2

Heidi Cullinan

for those lost at sea
may you soon dance upon the waves

Thanks to

Rebecca Lee for service dog help, and for being one of my most treasured friends, Nikki Hastings for beta reading and for being some of my favorite social media inspiration, Dan Cullinan for being the best assistant I've ever had, Anna Cullinan for being this book's in-house cheerleader urging me toward the finish line, Stephen Blackmoore and Kari for their cameo and giving Emmet & Jeremey a ride to the beach (buy Stephen's books!), and all my patrons, especially regencyfan93, Kelly Marilly Gonzalez, Sadie B, Katie M, Jennifer Harvey, Erin Sharpe, Sarah M, Sarah Plunkett, Ashley Dugan, Rosie M, Karin Wollina, and Pamela Bartual.

All rivers run to the sea, yet the sea is not full.

—King Solomon

CHAPTER ONE

Emmet

M Y BOYFRIEND, JEREMEY, thinks the moon looks like a watermelon.

He said this the night we visited my aunt for Christmas. My aunt who lives in Minneapolis, not the one who lives in Ames, though Althea was there that night too. Aunt Stacy has a telescope, and she let me use it to show Jeremey the moon up close. I was listing the names of the seas and craters when he told me what the moon reminded him of.

"It looks like a watermelon."

I tried to work out how the moon could be similar to a watermelon, but I couldn't do it. "Jeremey, it isn't even green."

"But it has the lines across it, the same as a watermelon, and they all come from a single point, the stub where the stem would have been, leading back to the rest of the plant. See? That spot there. The bright one at the bottom."

He let me use the telescope again. I still didn't see a watermelon. "That's Tycho. It's a crater."

"Like the toy company?"

"No. The toy company is spelled T-y-c-o. This is T-y-c-h-o, for the Dutch astronomer. It was seventy percent likely formed by the asteroid 298 Baptistina, which they used to think was the same one that made the dinosaurs go extinct, but then they found out it wasn't."

"It will always be a watermelon to me now. But I'll remember the stem's name is Tycho." Jeremey leaned on my shoulder, gazing at the moon without the telescope. "I didn't realize there were so many seas on the moon. I didn't think it had any water."

"It doesn't on the surface. Solar radiation burned all the water off, but they thought it might be in lunar rocks. Surface ice has been discovered recently, however."

"Why do scientists always look for water on the moon and other planets?"

"Because it's the essential element for any human habitation. Unfortunately, so far lunar habitation isn't looking good."

"But they have all those seas on the moon. Does that mean it used to have water?"

"No. Those are lunar maria, basaltic plains. The early astronomers thought they were ancient seas, but they were in fact formed by ancient volcanic eruptions."

Jeremey settled his head more heavily on my shoulder, listening, and so I kept talking. I told him about the lunar dust, how it covers the surface and comes from comets hitting the surface, five tons of dust rising and falling every day. How the dust takes ten minutes to land.

Jeremey shook his head. "What do you mean, ten minutes to land? That's how long until the dust hits?"

"No. It hits, then rises, but because there's so little gravity, it takes five minutes for it to rise and then five minutes to fall back down. Which means the moon has on average one hundred and twenty kilograms of lunar dust rising one hundred kilometers above the surface at all times."

"Wow. You know a lot about the moon."

I knew a lot more than what I'd said so far, and when I told him this, he asked to hear the rest. We sat there for another hour, me telling him everything I knew, until my voice was scratchy and I needed water. He went inside and got some for me, and then he talked while I drank it.

"It's so weird to think the moon has all those seas but no water. The names are so pretty. I almost prefer the Latin ones because they're so mystical. *Mare Nubium.* Though Sea of Clouds is nice too." He hugged his arms around his body. "Are there places on Earth called seas or oceans without any water?"

"They call the deserts sand seas, sometimes."

"That sounds sad, though."

He swayed back and forth, and I rocked and hummed with him because I was so content.

Then he spoke once more, his voice quiet. "I heard your mom talking inside. About The Roosevelt. Bob is worried about money."

I stopped rocking, but my insides felt jumbly the way they always did when this subject came up. The Roosevelt was the place where Jeremey and I lived, and Bob was the man who owned it, the father of David, one of our best friends. "David would tell us if something serious was wrong. Bob's having a fundraiser on New Year's Eve."

"Your mom is worried it won't be enough. Not with the budget cuts the state is proposing and the way they're restructuring the mental health system as a whole." Jeremey hugged himself tighter. "I don't want to lose The Roosevelt."

I didn't want to lose The Roosevelt either. I didn't think it was a good idea to worry, though. "Why don't we wait to talk to David. There's not much we can do about anything up here on the roof. We should enjoy the moon and think about how slowly the dust is rising and falling."

We did exactly that, and I noticed Jeremey relaxed. The next time he had something to say, it was about the moon, not about fears of losing our home. "Sometimes we say people have seas of emotion. What would *sea of emotion* be in Latin?"

"*Mare Adfectus*. And sand sea would be *Mare Ha-*

renam."

"I like *sand sea* in Latin better. But mostly I enjoy hearing you tell me all about things like the seas of the moon. Even if they are salt."

"Basalt isn't salt. It's silica."

"Can you tell me all about basalt and silica?"

I could, and I did.

Most people don't want to hear me talk about the things I know, but most people aren't Jeremey. He doesn't mind that I'm autistic. He says it's one of his favorite things about me. He says sometimes my autism is the best medicine for his depression and anxiety, which was why we'd gone up to the telescope in the first place. Jeremey was anxious in my aunt's house, and he'd been depressed for a few days as well, he'd told me. He'd been depressed more often than not for several months now, in fact, and it didn't matter how they adjusted his meds or how often he went to see his therapist, Dr. North. Depression, and sometimes anxiety too, kept getting the better of him. I wondered if it was because he was worried about the rumors we kept hearing about The Roosevelt being in trouble, though it was hard to say with depression. It could be for no reason except because depression eats happiness.

But Jeremey said when we sat together in the moonlight and I told him all the facts about the moon and basalt, he felt better.

Jeremey and I have been boyfriends for over two

years now. We've lived together for most of that time in The Roosevelt. Neither of us is okay to function in the world alone, but together and with the help of our friends and family, and the staff at The Roosevelt, we're independent and happy.

Except that night with Jeremey wrapped in a blanket and arranged carefully in my arms, I decided I didn't want to be quite so independent anymore. I wanted to keep Jeremey with me, to take care of him and to let him take care of me. I wanted to be dependent on him. I wanted him to be there to tell me the moon looks like a watermelon and then ask me to talk for another hour about basalt. I wanted to do everything with Jeremey, forever. This is a special kind of thing between boyfriends, when you feel this way. This meant I wanted to marry Jeremey.

With people on the mean, coming to such a realization would be simple. I would have bought a ring, asked him, and we'd have gotten married. But I'm not a person on the mean, and neither is Jeremey. And when I made the decision to marry Jeremey, it was only December. There were so many changes about to happen, earthquakes coming because the world wasn't content to let people such as Jeremey and me simply enjoy the next step in our happy ever after. Not without a lot of complications.

This story is about how we undid those complications and got ourselves the rest of our happy ever after anyway.

ASKING JEREMEY TO marry me was a big question, and it deserved some serious consideration and preparation. I knew getting married was complicated no matter what, but I didn't know what kind of accommodation my autism and his depression and anxiety would require from a practical standpoint. I was nervous, but not because I thought asking him was a mistake. Marrying Jeremey was a logical move, and I felt confident about our relationship. I didn't worry about Jeremey's answer, either. The probability of him saying no was low.

But I knew our families would be concerned, especially Jeremey's. They didn't like that I was autistic. They hated the autism part more than the gay part, Jeremey said. They would be upset if we got engaged, and this would upset Jeremey, which would only make his depression worse.

Jeremey's depression was often challenging for me. I had a difficult time understanding how to live with it as his partner. His anxiety was okay. He had the AWARE anxiety management strategy to manage himself, and I knew all the steps and could help him remember to do them. But depression was tricky. Anxiety I could see on the outside, but depression happened on the inside. It scared me. He'd already attempted suicide once, and I never wanted it to happen again. I knew I couldn't necessarily stop this from occurring, but I also knew the variables which influenced the odds.

My mother would call this splitting hairs. I will never understand either this metaphor or how anyone could split a hair with any knife or ax or sharp instrument of any kind.

There were other considerations to proposing to Jeremey, though. I didn't get disability anymore because of my employer, but Jeremey did. He had a job as our friend David's uncertified aide, but it was part-time. He attended community college for a short while to be a Certified Medical Aide, but it was too stressful for him. He took some classes online, but it was hard for him. Eventually he decided to stay on disability and maybe try classes another time. He made a small salary as David's aide, but it was basically a discount on his fees for being at The Roosevelt.

Right now his insurance comes from Medicaid, which is complicated and messy since the State of Iowa decided to make it privatized. My mother, a medical doctor, has a great deal to say about this, and most of it is swearing. All I know is when Jeremey had to switch to the private plan, he had to pick one of three insurance companies, and now he has to drive to Des Moines for half his appointments since most of the providers he used stopped taking his insurance due to the Medicaid privatization. Some of the doctors he saw only took one kind but not another, so he had to choose which ones he wanted to see. He has regular panic attacks over dealing with his health care management now, and this is with me, my parents, and The

Roosevelt staff helping him. My mother says people who don't have support staff are up "shit crick." *Crick* is a colloquial way of saying *creek*, which is a synonym for small stream. She assures me they do not actually need to walk up a river of poop, but they might as well because it would probably be less awful than navigating our new health system.

I've never been on Medicaid. Even if I had been, it wouldn't have mattered as we also had my family's insurance, which meant we could make other choices. Technically Jeremey could use his family's insurance until he is twenty-six, but then he would have to negotiate with his parents, who are challenging, so he's elected to deal with the messy state system alone. I don't use my family insurance anymore either, since I work full-time now at Workiva. I worked for them part-time while I was still in college because they think I'm a genius. This is because I *am* a genius.

Workiva gives me a generous salary and benefits package, including insurance. I thought if I married Jeremey, he could be on my insurance, but I didn't know if Jeremey's disability payments would change if he was my husband. Jeremey's job with David and his SSI payments cover his part of our bill for our apartment and fees at The Roosevelt with a tiny bit of spending money for Jeremey left over. The truth is if he didn't live with me, he couldn't afford to live at The Roosevelt. I don't know, to be honest, how he would live at all.

I hoped marrying me would make things easier, but it was worth checking to make sure they didn't get more complicated instead. The trouble was, I didn't know who to talk with about my plan. I thought about talking to David, who was my friend as much as Jeremey's, but he wasn't my first choice. David was disabled, but he wasn't on the spectrum. I felt these were spectrum issues, and so I decided I should go to a friend who was also on the spectrum, Darren.

I made the decision to contact Darren on my way home from work one day, so when I arrived at The Roosevelt, I was eager to go upstairs and begin the conversation. First, however, I had to stop in the lounge and say hello to Jeremey and my friends. I didn't want to because I was so focused on the potential conversation with Darren, but it would have been rude to skip them. Since the whole point was to figure out how to marry Jeremey, it was logical to take the time to care for his feelings first.

I was already being a good husband before I'd even proposed.

When the Workiva car dropped me off at The Roosevelt, I hummed, feeling happy. I liked that we had snow. Everything felt quieter when we had snow. There had been a blizzard the day before, and we'd made snow residents on the lawn. They smiled at me as I passed, and I smiled back.

As I entered the lounge, I counted seven people in the room, eight now because I was also present. David and Jeremey were there, as well as Sally and Tammy, the support staff for the building. Paul had his back to them as he played Xbox, but he had no headphones and the TV sound was off, so I knew he was listening to the conversation. Cameron was with Sally at the table, running his Spirograph while he spoke. This meant he was concentrating.

Stuart sat beside him, watching the circles and patterns and occasionally making yelp noises to let Cameron know he enjoyed the drawings and was excited to be included in the conversation. Most people wouldn't consider drawing a conversation, but it was to Cameron and Stuart.

Stuart is a strange guy. He's on the spectrum too—a lot of us in the building are—but there's something about him that makes me want to flap my hands. Technically the term for flapping is stimming, but I've always thought of it as flapping, so that's what I call it. Stuart makes me feel flappy. He uses his camera eyes to watch me, the same as I watch him. Like a lot of autistic people, he doesn't have to look directly at something to see it. Yet I always feel as if he's watching *me* whenever I'm in the lounge. Tammy says this is because I did a viral video with David and Jeremey last year. We dressed up like the Blues Brothers and danced through Target to Stuart's favorite song by his favorite artist, "Happy" by Pharrell Williams, and became YouTube stars for a few days. To this I say, why doesn't he watch Jeremey or David?

Tammy says it's because they don't dance like El-wood Blues or have autism the same as he does. Except our autism isn't the same, but Tammy doesn't understand. She means well, but autism isn't one size fits all. Stuart and I are living proof.

Beside Stuart was David in his wheelchair, and beside David was Jeremey. I signed my special hello to Jeremey, and then I flapped at the room so they knew I was happy to see them too.

Sally waved me over. "We're making plans for a party, Emmet. A New Year's Eve party. Come join us."

I ignored her for a minute because every time I see Jeremey after work I give him a touch. Jeremey loves touches and hugs about as much as they make me feel as if someone put my skin on inside out. Sometimes I hug him after work and sometimes I don't, but he always gets some physical contact from me.

I put a hand on his shoulder, and his body went soft as he leaned his cheek on my hand.

Though physical contact isn't my favorite thing as a general rule, when I touch Jeremey it's a different story. Today as it usually happened, when I rested my hand on his shoulder, I wanted to sign for him to go upstairs with me and have sex. But it would be rude to leave the party-planning meeting when I'd just arrived, plus I had the chat with Darren to do. So I found a straight-backed chair I could put near David and Jeremey.

David had waited to greet me because he knew Jeremey came first, but when I sat, he held out his fist for me to bump. Our fist bumps are awkward since I clunk too hard and he can't close his fist all the way or aim well to meet mine, but it's okay.

Tammy had a list in front of her with two columns, one labeled *activities* and another *snack food*. Karaoke and dancing were under the activities column. They were not my favorites. But Mexican train dominoes was on the list too, and I enjoyed this game a lot. I don't know what is Mexican about it, and I've asked, but Sally says it's only a name. I haven't been able to find any research that explains why it's called that either, but I enjoy the game a great deal.

I studied the snacks side of the list and flapped excitedly when I saw what she'd written. Parmesan popcorn was a treat Tammy made when she was extra happy or wanted to reward a resident. It was on the list twice, once with *plain* written beside it and the other saying there would be M&M's in the popcorn. This is because some residents enjoy the sweet and salty mixed together in the same bowl and some of us would need to go to the corner and hum if food were jumbled like that.

I didn't say much while the others planned. Too many people were talking at once, and work and thinking about how to propose to Jeremey had drained my energy, so when I had an idea, I sent texts to Jeremey, who read them to the group. But then I had a thought so big I wanted to say it myself. I tapped the table, and when Sally called on me, I said, "Can we invite Darren?"

"That sounds like a great idea. I'll talk to his staff and see about arranging for him to come over."

I was annoyed because I wanted to invite Darren myself, not have staff do it. I thought if I hurried to the apartment, I could maybe invite him first, but before I could excuse myself, Jeremey tapped my leg twice to get my attention. When I turned to him, he didn't speak, he signed.

A teacher of mine a long time ago taught me and my family to use American Sign Language to communicate during a period when speaking out loud felt too intense for me. I speak out loud often now, but I still use ASL sometimes because it's handy. My family, friends, and boyfriend use it too, especially when we wanted to have conversations without other people getting involved. When I saw what Jeremey had to say to me, I understood why he was signing instead of speaking.

I caught Sally and Tammy whispering about budgets in the staffroom when they didn't think I was close enough to hear.

Jeremey was worried about The Roosevelt closing again. Though if Sally and Tammy were whispering about it, maybe he was right to worry. I signed back to him. *We need to talk to David instead of eavesdropping.*

Jeremey nodded. *I thought I would go see him now before we went upstairs to make dinner. But it might mean we start making dinner and do our laundry late.*

This worked out perfectly. *I need to talk to Darren*

about something anyway. We can adjust our schedule by a half an hour or even forty-five minutes without a problem.

Jeremey smiled at me, and my chest felt warm and tight. *I love you, Emmet.*

I love you too, Jeremey.

I kissed the inside of my palm, then pressed that palm to Jeremey's. His eyes were bright as he took the kiss tight in his fist and his open palm to his lips.

I couldn't stop smiling. I loved him so much.

"I'll see you at dinner," I said, then stood to go get some advice on what would be the best way to marry him.

CHAPTER TWO

Jeremey

E MMET IS THE man I love, the only person I could ever imagine being with for the rest of my life. David Loris, however, is my best friend.

David and Emmet and I are all three best friends, really. People call us the Blues Brothers around town as a kind of local in-joke after our viral video, even though it bothered Emmet for a while as there were only two Blues Brothers in the movie and the *Saturday Night Live* skits. Honestly, I can't tell either of them this, but if it were up to me, I'd say the two of them could be John Belushi and Dan Aykroyd—David as Belushi and Emmet as Aykroyd—and I would be the guy with the camera or something. They're so funny and sharp and determined all the time, the ones who make all the plans. I...don't. David would say I was the quiet one, the stealth Blues Brother you had to watch out for, or something clever.

David is a C4 incomplete quadriplegic. This means

his spine is damaged at the C4 vertebrae, but it's not completely severed, which is important to understanding how his paralysis works. If he'd had a complete injury, he'd have no feeling whatsoever from those nerves on down, and there'd be no hope of repairing them with current medical technology. With an incomplete injury, however, how each patient experiences paralysis varies widely, and so does their recovery. David can use his left arm somewhat, but not his right, and he can feel parts of his legs on both sides, though he can't move either of them. I've seen him flick a toe on occasion, but he says he's not doing it. The movement is a nerve response. His nerves do odd things, jerking and twitching without him having any control over them, and he needs to be shifted in his chair manually because without those nerve pathways, his brain can't send the little signals to twitch and fidget and keep from getting sore that able-bodied people do literally without thinking about it.

Some of this kind of caretaking is my job. I wanted to go to school to be a certified nurse's aide so I could help David more, but school was too much for me and my anxiety, and I had to step out. David said it was no big deal, but I still feel like I failed him. I help him with daily tasks, though a lot of what I do is keep him company. He says that's worth more than I give myself credit for.

He must have thought I was having one of my low self-esteem moments as I escorted him back to his room, because when he saw my troubled expression, he gave me a very David grin and bumped my leg with his elbow when I reached for the handle to his door. "Hey. Don't hang around me when you've got your man waiting for you upstairs. I can handle opening my own doors."

"Actually, I wanted to talk to you about something. Can I come in for a minute?"

"Sure." He looked surprised and slightly nervous, turning his chair to face me as we entered the room. "What's up, J? Did I say something stupid to Train Man again? Do I need to go apologize?"

Train Man was David's nickname for Emmet. "No—you didn't do anything. I wanted ask about The Roosevelt." I bit my lip, feeling guilty, though I wasn't sure why. "Is it…is it in trouble? Money trouble?"

I had my answer in the way he tried to guard his expression. Eventually he gave up and sighed. "I'm not supposed to say anything, so don't tell anyone. But…yeah."

I have to tell Emmet, I wanted to point out, but I had a feeling David knew that was implied. My stomach twisted, and my throat felt thick and tight. "Is it…is it going to close?"

David shook his head, a rough, clumsy gesture because he was tired and his muscles were getting weak. "He won't let it close. But he has to find new funding. We're privately run, but everyone here gets money from state and federal programs, so in the end it's as if we're state-run anyway. Plus we got started the first few years on grants, and those have run out. And all these hospitals closing have fucked our shit."

I'd heard about the closings from Marietta, Emmet's mother. "The mental health facilities that closed, you mean? The hospitals and large-care institutions closing in favor of group homes?"

"Yeah, that bullshit. The state closed all of them. Like, *all* of them. There are floors of some hospitals, but that's it. Then there are group homes, and us. So you'd think, good business for The Roosevelt, right? *Nope.* They changed the way the law read, and you have to be a certain type of group home with a certain type of certification with a certain type of government contract. Dad about blew a gasket. What this boils down to is mental health services being sold off to corporations who don't give a shit about mental health, just business."

Now I understood why Marietta was so angry. "How can they do this?"

"The governor is a dick, is how, and in the last election people listened to a bunch of religious loonies and bigots, and now we have a conservative majority who—*surprise*—have no interest in anything but promoting corporate agendas. And since my dad isn't one of the corporate assholes in on the gravy train, we're screwed. We have no grants, none of these backroom-deal contracts, and fewer residents. There's no waitlist right now, and someone is moving out the first of the year. Which I didn't tell you about, but, so you know, it's happening."

The knot in my stomach tightened. "But you're sure The Roosevelt won't close?"

"I'm pretty sure my dad will move my family in here before he'd let things come to that, but yeah, money is tight. And getting tighter. What he's trying to do right now, as far as I know, is find better funding options. More workarounds on these stupid restrictions and asshole laws the governor wrote for his dickhead buddies who own managed care companies. He wants to lobby local lawmakers, that kind of thing. But it's getting hard for him to run his day job and keep The Roosevelt solvent too."

"Is there anything we can do? You and me, or any of us at The Roosevelt?"

David shrugged. "I don't know. I doubt it. I mean, I've thought about asking if I could go with Dad more to his fundraisers, but I hate being the crip on display, you know?"

"Yeah." I'd gone with David to a few of those fundraisers, and they were indeed pretty uncomfortable. David usually ended up on stage beside his dad, pasting on a smile while Bob got teary and talked about David's rehabilitation. Sometimes David told his own story, but it felt like a performance. As if everyone was there to watch a movie, to feel moved by David's trials and tribulations, make a donation, then go home. Meanwhile, this was David's life.

David grimaced. "I hate doing that shit, but if it's schmooze or close The Roosevelt, I'll do it."

I wasn't going to let him make the sacrifice alone. "I'll do it with you."

But my voice trembled as I said it, and David gave me a knowing look. "You're doing no such thing. You want to go barf up your sob story in front of strangers on a stage so they can masturbate to your pain, but you haven't told your boyfriend how bad your situation is yet?"

My cheeks got hot, and I averted my gaze. "How...how did you know I haven't told him?"

"Because he hasn't turned into a tornado of activity trying to help you." David leaned over as far as he dared in his chair and bumped me with his hand. "You've got to tell him. I know he's gonna freak out, but you've got to tell him how much worse your depression is. Pretty soon he's going to notice on his own, and then he's going to be worried and hurt both. He's already going to be upset he's the last to know."

I knew all of this and, ironically, it was making my depression worse. I wrapped my arms tight around myself and rocked, aware this was a habit I'd picked up from Emmet, the rocking as self-soothing. I wished I had told him a long time ago. I bit my lip and let a tear slide down my cheek. "Do you...think it's too late?"

"What, do I think he's going to break up with you over this? No. That's your depression talking. He might be mad, yes, but I think annoyed is more likely. Tell him why you held back. Then don't hold back anymore. And a bit of advice, bro: go tell him now. Get out of here and go do it. I need to take a nap anyway."

I wiped my eyes and stood, then went to David and hugged him. "Thank you."

He hugged me too, a quick but firm one-armed pat on my shoulder. "You're welcome. Now go. Don't worry about The Roosevelt, and don't worry about Emmet. Everything's going to be fine."

I did leave, but I worried too. About Emmet's reaction, and about the future of The Roosevelt.

I had a feeling I was going to worry about the future of The Roosevelt a lot.

CHAPTER THREE

Emmet

WHILE JEREMEY WENT to talk to David, I went to our room and invited my friend Darren to a Google Hangout.

Darren lives at Icarus House, a group home near the hospital. He's Jeremey's friend too because they'd been roommates while we waited for The Roosevelt to open. Darren is autistic, but his autism isn't the same as mine. He has other disabilities too, like our autistic hero Carly Fleischmann, that won't let him talk at all with his voice. He can whisper sometimes to videos, or make barking noises, or sometimes yell like he's a foghorn, but he says those noises bother him too. So usually he uses his computer to talk for him, or he signs.

Darren is a funny guy. He makes the best jokes. Also he is a panromantic asexual. He says most people don't know what it means. I do because I asked him, though I also Googled it. He says he's interested in romantic relationships, with any gender identity or orientation, for companionship, affection, and intimacy. However, he is not interested in sex and feels no sexual attraction whatsoever. He also does not care for most touch at all, especially not sexual touch, but he says he's curious about kisses from a philosophical and experimental standpoint.

I'm particular about who touches me and how, but I am definitely not asexual. I enjoy sex a great deal. Also, I am strictly gay.

Talking with Darren about asexuality is interesting. I hadn't heard about it until he told me he was asexual, but now I've done a lot of research and I feel more secure in my knowledge. I'm disappointed in how little information there is on non-binary and gray sexuality. Darren says this is because the world has a decided sexual bias. When he told me this, I pointed out the world probably has a sexual bias because of a biological imperative to procreate, and then we had a long debate about whether or not procreation was a necessary modern bias.

Darren is quite intelligent, but most people don't know this about him. Most people think he's the R-word and S-word autistic guy who hums and rocks on the couch while he whispers to his YouTube videos on his iPad. Except they don't say R-word and S-word. They say retarded and stupid. And dumb and moron and all the words I would never use about Darren or myself or any of my friends, anyone at The Roosevelt, anyone with a disability. Darren isn't any of those words. In fact, Darren is smarter than most of the people who call him names. He programmed his iPad to talk for him by writing his own app because the systems available for his family to order were too expensive. When we lived in the same town, we had a teacher who taught us American Sign Language to use for communication on days when speaking out loud felt like too much effort, but ASL was too tricky for Darren with his hands sometimes, so he modified ASL to be DSL, or Darren Sign Language. I learned it too, and the two of us can speak to each other in a code only he, a few teachers from junior high and high school, and his parents know. He took both the ACT and the SAT in high school, and while we both got perfect ACT scores, he got a 1550 on his SAT, and I only got a 1500.

Except he needed to take the test over several days, and it was only a practice test at home. He couldn't do the test in the testing center. It was hard for me to take it regularly with the other people, and I think it's why my score was a little low. I was lucky on my ACT because the testing center where I took it was empty that day and set up in an ideal way for me. Darren is more sensitive than I am, though. He needs to take tests in perfectly quiet rooms with headphones on or something to decrease the stimuli, and he needs breaks. But according to people on the mean, this is cheating.

Even if Darren could have taken the tests in the

center, it would have been difficult for him to go to college. His family doesn't have any money. They did for a while, but then his dad lost his job at Amana Manufacturing when it got bought by Maytag, and his mom got sick. She's better now, but between Darren's health issues and hers, and his dad's unemployment due to severe depression, they don't have any money.

I knew Darren when we were in junior high, when we both lived in Iowa City, before my family moved to Rochester, Minnesota. Darren's family still lives in Iowa City, but Darren came to Icarus House a few months before I met Jeremey. The group home he'd been living in closed, and when he heard Dr. North— my therapist and Jeremey's too—had relocated to Ames, Darren asked to be transferred to a facility here instead. He and I rediscovered each other when Darren and Jeremey became roommates for a brief time after Jeremey left the hospital, after Jeremey's suicide attempt but before we moved into The Roosevelt.

Now Darren and I speak to each other regularly, and today I was about to speak to him again. I planned to use chat, and I could have used my phone, but I wanted to use my computer because I like the feel of the keyboard.

We didn't use video as neither of us needs faces to talk. When he logged on, I greeted him.

Hello, Darren, I typed. *This is Emmet.*

I rocked while I waited for him to respond. He types slowly because his fingers don't listen to his brain the same as someone's on the mean or even as quickly as mine.

Hello, Emmet. This is Darren. What's up?

I had two things to talk to him about now, and I didn't know which to talk about first. I decided the party was best, because talking about marriage felt complicated.

We're having a New Year's Eve party, and I asked if we could invite you. Tammy will talk to your staff to see if you can come, but I wanted to invite you myself first. We will have games and snacks. I will play Mexican train dominoes with you all night if you want. Staff can help you move the dominoes.

I realized Stuart might try to play, which made me frustrated.

It will be a very good game. Also they will have brownies. I said this because Darren doesn't care for popcorn, but he loves brownies and cake. I would ask my mom to make the brownies if staff didn't make them.

I stopped typing and waited for him to reply. The pause was extra long, so I knew Darren was thinking. Eventually, he replied.

I would like to come, but I probably can't stay long. The staff at Icarus won't want to come get me after the shift change. They cut the budget again, but after the state closed all those residential hospitals we're also overcrowded. I have two room-mates right now. They snore and break all my things.

The Roosevelt was a group home in a way, same as Darren's, but where I lived was privately funded. Icarus House was publicly funded and didn't have much money or staff. I visited Jeremey there and I didn't think it was a good place. Many of the residents are loud and the couches smell bad. Darren doesn't like it, but he doesn't have any money, only what disability gives him. My mom says places such as The Roosevelt are rare and precious, and not many people have money enough to pay for a family member to live there. Worse, most people with disability can't keep regular jobs, if they can have them at all. I make lots of money, enough to pay my way and my boyfriend's, and I still have some savings left over. But most people here, even high-functioning autistic people, don't have jobs like mine.

I wished Darren could live somewhere rare and precious too. I wished he could live down the hall from Jeremey and me.

Maybe you could stay overnight at The Roosevelt, I typed.

Where would I sleep?

A tricky question. *You could stay in my room. I could sleep with Jeremey.*

That would be too hard for you. Maybe ask Jeremey if he would let me borrow his room and he could sleep in your room.

This was almost as difficult for me as giving my room to Darren. We were boyfriends but have two rooms because sometimes I need my own space. Jeremey in my space was okay, but if there was a problem and I needed to be alone, I couldn't if Darren was using Jeremey's room. But it was a better idea. Jeremey would sleep on the couch if I needed space. *I will ask Jeremey if he will let you borrow his room for one night. Would you be okay in a new place?*

It would be strange, but Icarus House isn't good either. It will be a strange thing for a bad thing. That's all.

His point was logical. I could always count on Darren for logic. *Okay. I will ask and text you.*

I hadn't asked him what he thought about how to propose to Jeremey, but I felt unsure about bringing this up now, so I decided to wait for later and ended our chat. I sat in my rocking chair in the living room, rocking and looking out the window. It was dark outside, so I kept the lights in our apartment low so I could see a train if it went by. None did, though, and soon Jeremey was home.

He smiled as he gave me a good-evening kiss, and then we made dinner together. We do this every night, usually at six though it was later tonight of course since we'd altered our schedule so Jeremey could talk to David and I could talk to Darren.

We make our dinner from fresh, not a box. Every Sunday my mom takes us shopping and helps us measure out all the ingredients we'll need for the whole week. Tonight was vegan macaroni and cheese with broccoli. It uses a cashew cheese sauce my mom makes at home and puts in the fridge for us. All we have to do is boil the pasta, add the sauce and chopped broccoli, and bake it for twenty-five minutes.

Normally I don't care to talk while we make meals except to ask Jeremey to pass me something or point out he's doing something the wrong way, but while our dinner baked I told Jeremey about my conversation with Darren. He agreed it would be good for Darren to come for the whole night, and he also agreed with Darren's suggestion for a sleeping arrangement.

"I'd be more than happy to lend him my room for the night. And don't worry. If you're overwhelmed after the party and need to be alone, I'll sleep on the couch." He hugged his arms closer and rounded his shoulders, and he made a sad face too. "I wish Darren could live at The Roosevelt. He's right, Icarus is awful. It's not bad in a dangerous way, but it's horribly depressing."

I remembered how depressed Jeremey had been while he lived there. My mom had said it wasn't because of Icarus House, just because of depression, but I don't think Icarus House helped much. I rocked in my chair and hummed. My brain was still thinking about getting married, but now it was thinking about Darren living in The Roosevelt too. An idea was building in my mind, and I'd learned at work sometimes I could help ideas come out if I let out noises. The woman who works across the hall can hear me when I make them, but she says she doesn't mind because it's the same as when she's doing some kind of yoga breathing.

This idea was tricky, though, and it needed dark and quiet. I looked at the timer. "Jeremey, would you mind watching our dinner and finishing setting the table? I want to go to my closet."

Jeremey blinked. "Sure. Is everything okay?"

"Yes. I would like to think about an idea I have to help Darren."

Jeremey made a surprised-happy face. "Oh, great—please, go to your closet. And actually, how about you take whatever time you need? I can turn the oven to warm when it's done, until you're ready."

I worried leaving it in the oven would make the macaroni crunchy, which I find unpleasant. "Will you please put foil over it first?"

He said he would, so I went to my closet to see if I could hum enough to let the idea in my head come out and help Darren.

MY BEDROOM HAS a closet, but I don't keep clothes in it. They let me wear whatever feels comfortable at Workiva, and that clothing can go in a dresser drawer. The few nice things that must hang Jeremey lets me keep in his room. The closet in my room is empty, and it doesn't have shelves or a bar because Bob, David's dad and the owner of The Roosevelt, took them down for me. My closet is my safe space, full of pillows and blankets and my sensory sack.

Many autistic persons enjoy sensory sacks, which are composed of Lycra and can stretch or hug close, depending on how you push on the material. Sometimes I like to roll around the bed in mine, but usually I use it in my therapy closet. I wrap it close to my body, curl up in the dark, and shut out all stimuli. I usually hum too, either to calm or to focus.

Today I climbed in my sack and hummed. Working at Workiva has taught me how to focus. They let me design my office the way I needed it to be and helped me figure out how to make it better. My office is blue because blue means ocean, which is a thing between me and my boyfriend. Oceans are not actually blue. It's just the reflection of the sky. But I've studied metaphor and symbolism, and it's okay. I can pretend oceans are blue. Especially since I would have had to hire an artist to paint my walls all the colors an ocean actually is, and Workiva is understanding but not that understanding.

They had a seminar one day about how to have better work habits, and one of the things they talked about was how to respect the flow of ideas. They talked about ideas being feathers, but I don't think it's a good metaphor. Ideas are basically mind robots. They're constructed inside your mind and then move around to build more things. Sometimes they leave your head and go collect information, but usually they stay and whisper while they connect wires and build structures. They're difficult to hear and to see. But if I hum the right way, sometimes I can tune in to their frequency. I don't think they use radio waves, but whatever waves they do use, I can hear them better if I hum the right note at the right volume. So I got in my sack and hummed until I could find the ideas whispering about how I could help my friend Darren.

I have hummed a lot about marrying Jeremey, but feelings *do* behave like feathers and gum up the idea robots and make a big mess. I have a lot of feelings about marrying Jeremey. Nothing gets done when I think about marrying Jeremey.

The problem for Darren and his living arrangement, the ideas told me, was Darren didn't have money. Other people had money, but the people had to be connected to Darren or they wouldn't give him money. I whispered to the ideas what kinds of connections I knew about—family and friends—but the ideas said friends weren't the same. Usually friends don't give that kind of money. It needed to be a lot of money, and friends were usually only willing to give a little money for a short while.

"But Jeremey is my friend, and I'll give him money for a long time. Forever." Unless I died before him, which was troubling. I hummed a different note while I thought about that.

This made feathers get in the way and the ideas got angry, so I put worrying about dying on an invisible shelf in my closet and went back to humming about ideas to help Darren.

I didn't need the ideas to point out it was different to help a boyfriend than it was to help a friend. I would be happy to help Darren, but I didn't make enough money to help two people and take care of myself. I would if I never went shopping, but I need toothpaste, and I only like Biotene, which is an expensive tooth-paste. I could help him some, though.

There were 58,965 people living in Ames. I didn't need very many of them to help Darren in order for him to stay at The Roosevelt. I wondered how I could contact them and convince them to share their money.

I hummed for a long time, but I never solved the problem, and eventually my stomach complained that I needed to get out of my closet and go eat. When I went into the kitchen, it was half an hour after the macaroni should have been done.

Jeremey got up from the table, putting down his iPad as I came into the kitchen. "I didn't want the macaroni to get crunchy, so I called your mom, who told me I could put a damp towel under the foil, once the oven was turned to warm, and it worked!"

I was excited to hear I didn't have to eat crunchy macaroni and happy Jeremey had taken care of me. He was already a good husband too. I kissed his cheek to let him know, because it's important to Jeremey to have people hear they appreciate him. "Can we eat now?"

Jeremey didn't ask me about my time in the closet while we ate, as I dislike talking during a meal, but when I put my napkin on the table to show I was finished eating, he asked me questions. "How did it go? Did you think of anything to help Darren?"

"No. The problem is money. He needs a lot of money for a long time to live here. I don't know how to find this kind of funding."

"Right. We could maybe help raise enough money for a short while, but if he couldn't keep up enough money, he'd have to return to Icarus House. Or somewhere worse."

It was a good thing my mom wasn't in the room. She'd yell about how the governor was selling the poor and disabled down the river. This was another metaphor I will never understand. Who would you pay to send someone down a river, and which river would you use and why, but I do know it means doing bad things to people. I stopped thinking about rivers and governors and focused on the problem of Darren. "He needs a job. He's smart. There should be a job for him somewhere."

"He *is* very smart. And he's a very nice man. What are his superpowers, besides camera eyes?"

Jeremey and I talk about people's superpowers being the things they're good at, better than other people. "Darren is good at math. He's good at finding things on the Internet too. Better than me."

"That's impressive, because you're *amazing* at finding things on the Internet." He leaned back in his chair. "There has to be a job for someone with skills like his. Did Darren go to college?"

"No. He's taken a lot of online classes, though, especially the free ones." I did my best to think of jobs I'd heard of that Darren could do. He works at the library, but it's only a part-time job and doesn't pay very much. He wouldn't ever be able to go to an office like Workiva. He could work remotely, which I could do also but don't care to because I prefer my workspace. But Darren would need a special driver and a helper to get to his workspace, and then he'd need to stay late in order to get his work done, since he works slowly.

As I've watched my friends search for employment, I've come to understand my experience in finding a job at Workiva is highly unusual for someone with disabilities. Or rather, the reason a successful company was willing to give me a high-paying job was due to the desirable skills that come with my disabilities, skills these companies need. Also, the company that hired me is known for working outside the mean in unusual systems and environments. Normally employment for people with disabilities is granted as a favor or out of pity, if it is provided at all, and it is offered in a separate space, with a lower level of pay.

We aren't usually allowed to work with people on the mean on an equal level the way I am. Despite my autism, I can, if I apply myself, appear to be like people on the mean. Darren cannot, not once he moves or attempts to speak. Not when he tries to keep up with the pace of people on the mean, despite having skills they can never hope to possess.

It's not fair, and it isn't right, but it's a problem without an answer inside my sensory sack or any other place I know how to find. I didn't know how to help Darren.

"I'll talk to David about it," Jeremey said. "But in the meantime, Darren can come to the party, and that will be a good start."

I thought so too.

Jeremey bit the edge of his lip. "I talked to David about The Roosevelt. About whether or not it's in trouble." He pushed the napkin under his plate and bit harder on his lip. "He told me it is."

I sat up straighter in my chair. "Is it going to close?"

Jeremey shook his head. "No, but it needs more money, and Bob is running out of ideas on how to get it."

I hummed and flapped for a moment. "I'll spend some time in my sensory sack later and see if I can think of something." Though it occurred to me I had so many things to think about in my sensory sack now I was going to have trouble working it into my schedule. And as much as I loved Darren and The Roosevelt, I wasn't giving up the time I saved for taking showers or having sex. Dr. North says self-care is important.

We did the dishes, and then because it was Monday, we did laundry. We have our own washer and dryer in a tiny room between our bedrooms, and we wash our clothes together. The washer is front load with a glass door, and I like to sit on a pillow in front of it and hum while I watch the clothes spin.

Tonight while I sat, Jeremey put his head in my lap. It's a lot of touch, but Jeremey lies still, so it's a pleasant, heavy pressure. For him it's important touch, and I enjoy studying him as he lies there. Sometimes when he does this I look at him as much as I look at the washer, my camera eyes seeing both.

"Emmet?" Jeremey's voice was soft, almost sad. "I need to tell you something, but I'm afraid to tell you."

I stopped paying attention to the washer and put all my attention on Jeremey. I tried to read his face, but it was complicated and impossible. I study flash cards of which facial expressions correspond to which emotions, but some are too much to put on a card. "Please don't be afraid to tell me things. I love you."

"I know." Jeremey put his hand on my knee and squeezed. A tear ran out of his eye, over the skinny part of his nose and onto my pants. "I don't want to say it out loud. It will feel more real if I say it out loud."

"Feelings aren't facts." This is a thing Dr. North says often. "Also, if it's true, it won't be any different if you say it out loud or not."

More tears fell, but Jeremey remained still. Too still. My stomach felt queasy, because I knew exactly what was wrong with Jeremey, what he didn't want to tell me. I hummed and rocked, flapping my hands to send some of the fear away, but it didn't work. I was still scared.

"Jeremey, is your depression bad?"

His expression still wooden, Jeremey nodded.

I hummed and rocked and flapped more. "Is it bad? Worse than at Christmas?"

He nodded once more.

I flapped so much my fingers snapped together. It calmed me, made the buzzing in my ears not so loud. I asked the question I feared the most, the thing I was most afraid of in the whole world. "Jeremey, do you want to kill yourself again?"

Jeremey was still a long time. I held my breath, watching him with my camera eyes. Finally, he shook his head, and I breathed out.

"But I can feel it." Jeremey kept squeezing my knee. I didn't mind because it was a hard touch, and it reminded me he was there. "It's not a voice, but when the depression is heavy and I get tired, it's as if I can see this pond and I know if I went into it, I'd feel peace."

"No. You would feel dead."

"I know. But when I'm depressed, it's difficult to remember." He bit his lip, and more tears came out. "I talk to David about it sometimes. But it's different for him. His depression isn't the same as mine." He let go of my knee and wiped at his tears, but more came as soon as he swept those away. "I feel so lonely all the time. Which is stupi—"

"You can't use the S word," I reminded him. We didn't say the R word or the S word. Ever.

"It doesn't make sense to be lonely. I'm with people all day long. Dr. North says it's different, that lonely isn't the same as being alone, but…I still feel st—silly. And lonely. And sad. I try not to be. I try to be happy.

But inside I'm not."

I felt sad now too. I hadn't known my boyfriend was this unhappy. He had seemed happy to me while we made dinner. Maybe I hadn't been paying attention. Maybe I wasn't a good almost husband after all.

"Have you talked to Dr. North about your depression being worse?"

"Yes. He asked me to try some alternative therapies in addition to some new medications. He wants me to run to get my adrenaline up, but I don't want to do that. I'd have to go in the neighborhood alone. People might talk to me. Or think I was rude for avoiding them."

Jeremey also had social anxiety. He was fine when he was with me or with David, but alone was never a good plan for him. "My mom used to have a treadmill in the basement. She could maybe bring it over here. Or you could go over there. My parents' house isn't far."

"I don't... Not yet. It's too much. I'm sorry." He sighed. "This was another thing he asked me to do. Vocalize my struggles with my depression to you. So at least I've done that."

I wasn't sure how vocalizing helped Jeremey's depression. Maybe, though, it was good because now *I* could help. Probably me helping hadn't been what Dr. North meant. He'd gone to school a long time and knew more about depression, but it didn't mean I couldn't do something too. "I'll do some research and see if there are some alternative therapies that might be better suited to you. If you like some of them, you can ask Dr. North if he thinks they're good therapies."

More tears fell from Jeremey's eyes. I could reach the tissue from the box on the table beside the sofa from where we were sitting, and so I took one to dry Jeremey's tears, but when I wiped his face, Jeremey caught my hand and kissed my fingers. "I'm sorry I took so long to tell you my depression was worse."

I touched his lips. "You don't need to be sorry."

He squeezed my hand. "I thought you might be angry because I didn't tell you right away."

I didn't understand why he thought I would be angry, but I did feel sad that Jeremey had worried I would be angry. I shook my head. "I would never be angry at you about being depressed, Jeremey. Only sad because I couldn't take it away for you."

He shut his eyes, the lines on his face relaxing. "Thank you, Emmet. You're the best boyfriend ever."

I was pretty sure the best boyfriend ever would have known his boyfriend was depressed without being told, but I didn't say this, only kept wiping Jeremey's face and humming as we sat together, listening to the washer finish its cycle.

CHAPTER FOUR

Jeremey

THE NIGHT I confessed to Emmet my depression had become bad again, I lay awake late into the evening, staring at the ceiling of my bedroom, thinking about treadmills.

Emmet was the third person in as many days to suggest I use one. Three times people had told me treadmills were the perfect solution to my problem, and three times I had smiled and nodded instead of replying, "I fucking hate treadmills." I would never have spoken so rudely to Emmet because it would have upset him, but it was with him I came the closest to blurting out the truth. I wanted to tell him treadmills made me crazy. They didn't go anywhere, and I loathed them for it. This was my whole life, staying in place, rehashing the same shit. I didn't need exercise equipment to reinforce this.

Also, treadmills were so rigid. If I got tired, they didn't give a damn. They kept going. I know that was

the point, but I didn't appreciate it. If I had to run, which I couldn't say I was a fan of, I wanted to be outside, in the trees. I wanted to go *somewhere*, even if it was only around a block. Maybe it would be the same block over and over, but it would never be the same block every day. Different cars would be parked on it. Different people would pass by.

I wished I could guarantee no one would stop and talk to me while I walked. I could get exercise, would happily add walking as part of my therapy—jogging, whatever I needed to do—but whenever I tried, all that happened were strangers insisted on striking up conversation. Even if I had headphones on, they wanted to get chatty. If I had David with me, it was a little better, but his chair took up the whole sidewalk, and anyway, *he* loved talking to people.

I rolled to my side in the bed, bunching the blanket tight so I could hug it to my body. I was exhausted, so worn out I could barely move, and yet I couldn't sleep because my brain was a hamster wheel. Depression clawed at me, a yawing spiral beneath my feet, and it left me so weary, but anxiety chewed at my insides, thrilled to have me captive at last so it could feast. It told me to call myself the S word for not liking treadmills or being able to run in the neighborhood, for making such a big deal out of a simple thing such as getting exercise. It told me I was right, I should hate that this was my life, how I couldn't be happy like everyone else. I could hear, dimly, the voice of my

therapist reminding me everyone else wasn't happy, everyone had problems, but I argued with the voice. Yes, everyone had problems, but they didn't have *these* problems.

Thanks to my fucking brain chemistry, I was going to spend the rest of my life weeping in the kiddie pool while everyone else sighed about the difficulties of the deep end and the super slide. It made me angry. Sad.

Made me feel so *alone*.

My depression was bad now, worse than before I'd confessed to Emmet. It was ever-present lately, this thing I was always aware of, but I'd hoped telling him would make it better, that saying it existed would lessen its effect. Talking about it hadn't changed anything. I felt like I was clinging to the edge of a pit, sand whipping around my face, the wind swirling below and trying to suck me into the darkness.

I thought of lying in bed for eight more hours, spending the whole time fighting not to let go and slide in, knowing the whole time I'd also be battling the whispers predicting terrible things might happen to me. Technically I knew I was capable of such a fight. I also knew it meant I would be a pile of pudding the next day. If I wanted any chance of functionality tomorrow, I was going to need to take one of my pills, the ones I hated, the ones that made the pit go away, but I went away too.

The pills would give me a hangover. If I took one now, I'd lose part of tomorrow. Through noon, most

likely. I might get the afternoon. Maybe the morning if I pushed. Even with all this, though, it would be a dull, flat day.

Why was this my life? How was this fair? Why couldn't I climb out of this pit? Why couldn't I enjoy my life? Why was this how I had to exist?

The dark whispers tugged at me, pulling at my feet. Part of me simply floated there in the middle of nowhere, waiting for it to end. Part of me clawed harder at the edge.

Oh God, I was cycling. And slipping. I needed one of my pills, right now.

Where *were* my pills?

I opened my eyes, lifted my head. I felt as if someone had filled me with cement. The pills weren't on my bedside table. The only thing I saw was a pile of tissues and my phone, which I'd forgotten to plug in. Left to my own devices, my room would be a mess, and my med bottle would have been on my bedside table but now probably knocked off and rolled under the bed or lost under moldy laundry. However, I live with Emmet Washington. He comes in every evening and helps me tidy up. The only reason tissues littered my nightstand was because I'd been crying as I went to sleep, and I'd had to blow my nose.

But where were my meds? I tried to think. My head hurt, both from crying and from exhaustion. My head was also somehow seventy-five pounds heavier than usual. *Think, think...*

I remembered, the thought blooming like the scene from a movie in my mind. Hall closet by the bathroom. I could see the med basket, the tidy box labeled with my name. It was just outside the door. Emmet's mother said it wasn't good to keep medication in the bathroom because of the moisture from the shower, so we kept our medicine in the hall closet. So that was great, I knew where it was. Except as heavy as my body felt, as intense as the depression was on me, the damn meds might as well have been on the moon. The idea of pushing back my covers, leaving the bed, walking across the room, opening the door...I was exhausted simply thinking about it.

I knew what I needed to do, but I didn't want to do it. I'd only had to do this a few times before, but having to ask on the heels of my confession felt so crude. I felt like an animal, or something worse. Shame licked at me as I fumbled with my phone and texted Emmet.

help pls

I heard him leave his bed, open his door, open mine.

"Jeremey?" His voice, scratchy from sleep, pierced the dark.

I couldn't look at him, too ashamed, only stared at my phone, still in my hand, tears falling down my face. "I'm sorry. I...need my pills. I...can't."

He came to stand beside my bed. "Which pills? Are you hurting? Do you need ibuprofen?" He rocked back and forth, and his hands flapped gently. I'd scared him.

"Klonopin." There. Now I'd scared him more.

He left without a word. I heard him in the hallway, searching for the bottle, then in the kitchen, getting a glass of water. When he returned to the bedroom, I pushed myself to a sitting position. It felt as if I'd moved a mountain of earth. I was able to keep myself upright, but my head felt heavy, and my shoulders rolled forward, burdened by my self-disgust. My arms shook, and my torso slumped, as if my spine couldn't support itself. "I'm sorry," I whispered.

"Why are you sorry?" He held the water and the pill out for me, staring at the top of my hair with a mildly puzzled expression, but I knew how to read Emmet's face. He was worried, terribly so. "Please take your medicine so you can feel better."

"It won't make me better. It'll make me feel like a cotton ball." I had unusually strong reactions to a lot of medication, and this was one of them. But better a cotton ball than a sand pit of death, so I took the pill anyway, and the water. "I hate this. I hate that I have to be this way."

"I don't hate you this way. I love you." Emmet sat beside me and took my hand in his awkward, Emmet manner. "The depression is telling you lies right now."

It was. I knew this, but... "It's always telling me lies, Emmet. And it's so much work to tell it to stop talking, to not listen."

"Do you want me to sleep in here with you to-night?"

Longing struck me like an arrow. I wanted it more than anything, but… "You had a stimulating day. You wanted to sleep alone."

He hummed and rocked. "You're having a bad time with depression. You need your partner. A relationship is about compromise. It's my turn to compromise."

A sob rose out of nowhere, lodging in my nose. I held it back like a sneeze, shutting my eyes tight. *Here it is.* The thing I feared most. And I was so tired, so busy keeping myself from falling into despair, I couldn't keep the confession from tumbling out of my mouth. "But if you have to compromise too much, you'll leave me, and then I won't have anyone."

Emmet squeezed my hand tight. "I will never leave you. I love you."

Why was he deliberately not understanding me? Was he pitying me? The darkness dared me to let him see it. *Push him away now. It'll hurt, but you're already hurting. Won't it be easier to deal with that hurt now too?* "But you can't love this. Nobody can love *this*."

He was humming now, his free hand flapping. "What do you mean, this? You? Yes, I do love you. I just said so. I don't understand."

I gave up. "You want me to spell it out? Fine. *My depression.* That *this.* You can't love my depression. Nobody can. I certainly don't. But it's a part of me. I can't get rid of it."

I hadn't meant to blurt it out, but this is the thing with being with Emmet. He doesn't understand subtlety, and so you end up being blunt when you don't mean to be, don't want to be. I hunched forward farther, but there wasn't any escaping my exposure now. I was in the pit. I *was* the pit.

Soft lips pressed to my cheek, cool dampness startling me out of my vortex of despair. I turned toward him, and Emmet kissed me again, this time on the lips.

"If your depression is part of you, then I love it too."

I wanted to argue with him, to tell him he was only saying that and didn't mean it, but it's difficult to do deny someone when you're getting kissed. When your boyfriend is holding you close and whispering over and over he will take care of you, saying you should lie down and let him hold you. When the first tendrils of your super drug are leaching into your brain, turning you into a pile of cotton candy.

Except before the drug untethered me from the edge of my vortex, something changed. As I lay there in bed, my whole body engulfed by Emmet's, his face pressed into the back of my neck, his breath a rhythmic echo in my ear, I still felt the edge of the pit. But this time, all around me, instead of the sucking blackness of the void, I felt the warm, sheltering presence of my lover's arms.

CHAPTER FIVE

Emmet

I HADN'T FALLEN asleep until three in the morning the night Jeremey told me his depression was bad again. I'd been tossing and turning in my own bed when he'd texted me, but once I saw how upset he was, I was upset too. I'd meant what I told him about compromise, but it was still true that I'd had too much stimulation. Now I'd had more. Sleep was impossible.

So I lay there holding Jeremey, watching him sleep instead. I counted the hairs on his head until I got lost and my eyes hurt from straining in the dark. I noticed the pattern of cotton on his T-shirt, the way the fiber of the collar was thicker than the main part.

I pressed my nose into Jeremey's hair, my mouth to his neck, taking deep breaths to fill my body with the smell of him, trying to find the molecules of depression inside him so I could take them apart and better understand them too. But I could not. Not even when I stuck my tongue out and licked his skin.

The only way I was able to sleep was when I rocked, cradling Jeremey's body to mine and swaying the two of us until it exhausted me. I don't remember becoming unconscious, but the next thing I knew, my alarm was going off in the other room, and this one was full of sun.

Jeremey was still in my arms, asleep. He stirred slightly when I rose, but not much. The drug did that to him. He would sleep all day if we let him, and I wanted to let him.

I couldn't sleep, though, and my lateness had already thrown my day off schedule. It had taken ten minutes for me to hear my alarm since I was in the wrong room. Normally I wake up, shower, get dressed, eat toast, drink tea, eat oatmeal and an egg, brush my teeth, kiss Jeremey goodbye, then go to work. If I want to have sex with him before I go to work, I set my alarm an extra half hour early. But today I was off my schedule, and I had more on my schedule. I had to tell someone about Jeremey. I was upset. Too upset even for sex. I had to think of what to do.

I sat in my rocking chair, humming and flapping as I stared out the window and thought for several minutes. Then I called the man who drove me to my job at Workiva every day.

"Hello, Tom, this is Emmet Washington. I will be late to work today. I have a family situation. I apologize."

"Oh, I'm sorry to hear that. Do you need a day

off?"

I considered this. I hadn't missed work at all, except for vacation days, which had always been planned. I hadn't even been sick. If I stayed home, I could help Jeremey. But if I didn't go to work, I'd feel bad for the other members of my team, because my absence would mean they'd have to do my work unexpectedly. "I don't know if I need a day off. I would like to stay home, yes. My boyfriend is having a bad day with depression. I didn't sleep much last night. I'm worried about him."

"Oh, kiddo. You need to call in. I can tell your supervisor for you, have him call you, if you want."

I thought I should be the one to call my supervisor, and I thought I should point out I was not a kiddo, but at the same time, I was quite tired. The idea of not going to work, of going to bed, was incredibly appealing. I could get into my sensory sack and sleep. My day would be disjointed and off schedule, but I'd be with Jeremey, and this was what mattered. "Thank you, Tom."

Tom chuckled. "Not a problem. Text me later, okay, and let me know about tomorrow? And give my love to Jeremey."

I hung up, then stared at my phone, wondering what to do now.

I was hungry but also tired. I spun my schedule backward, trying to decide if I needed to take care of anything else. I couldn't think of anything, though it was possible I was too tired to see it. I would eat cereal, then sleep. But a thought kept nagging at me, telling me there was something else I needed to do.

Then it hit me. David. Jeremey was supposed to go to work too, with David.

I texted him, not sure if he was awake yet or not. *Hello, David, this is Emmet. Jeremey had a bad night. I am staying home from work to be with him. I am going to eat cereal then go to sleep. He took a Klonopin, so he is extra sleepy too. He will probably not be able to be your aide today.*

I sent the text, and within a minute my phone rang, the caller ID and the vibration pattern telling me it was David. I answered. "Hello, David. This is Emmet."

"Hey, Train Man. Is Jeremey okay?"

"No. He had a bad night. The depression is worse. He said he told you." He'd confessed it to David before me, which I didn't like, but I wasn't going to bring this up right now.

"I know, but that's not what I meant. I just…" He sighed. "I hate this for him."

I did too. "I'm going to take care of him."

"I'm glad he was finally able to tell you. He was letting his fear run away with him, worrying his depression would turn you away."

"I would never turn Jeremey away." I was annoyed people kept thinking this.

"I know you wouldn't. I think he does too, deep down. He's afraid, is all. Don't you fear he'll leave you, sometimes?"

All the time. "I do."

"It's what people in love do at first, I think. Not that I'd know."

Finding David a girlfriend was on my list of things I wanted to do, but first I had to help Jeremey. And Darren. Also I had to sleep. I had too many things to do and not enough sensory sacks to do them in. "I need to eat and go to bed."

"You go eat and sleep. But thanks for letting me know. I'll stop up later and help, if you want. And don't worry about helping me. I'll get by on my own."

David did need Jeremey's help, I knew, but like me, he was compromising. "Thank you, David."

"Anytime, buddy."

I was glad to be off the phone. I ate my cereal and went to my room to get my sensory sack, but instead of climbing into my bed to sleep, I carried it to Jeremey's room and spread it on the bed beside him. I zipped it so most of my body was inside but my head was still out, so I could feel Jeremey's hair on my face while I slept.

The next time I woke, Jeremey was out of bed. He'd moved to the living room and curled up on the couch watching television under a blanket. He smiled at me when I came out, but I could see the drug in him, making him watery. He muted the show when I came to sit across from him.

"How are you feeling?" I asked.

"Better." He pushed himself more upright in his

pile of blankets. "Why aren't you at work?"

"I took the day off so I could be with you." It had seemed so important before, but now, sitting with him, I worried whether or not it was okay.

His expression softened. "Oh…you didn't have to do that for me. But thank you."

"Also I was tired from not sleeping. But I was worried about you and wanted to be here to help you." I rocked back and forth on the ottoman. "Can you tell me how I can help you?"

Jeremey tugged his blanket around himself. "I…don't know. I guess I'm better, but the drug makes me so foggy. Everything is so much work. Even getting myself food is hard."

I stood up. "I can get you food. What do you want to eat?"

Jeremey bit his lip. "Um, a sandwich? Maybe soup?"

"I can make you both. Would you like a turkey sandwich with lettuce and Swiss cheese and mayonnaise, and tomato soup with milk? And some crackers?"

I loved the way he smiled at me. When he looked at me that way, he made me feel as if I could hold up the whole world with one hand. "A soup and sandwich would be so nice. Thank you, Emmet."

I brought him the sandwich and the soup, and I got him a Sprite too. Normally we only eat in the dining room so it doesn't make a mess, but I brought him the food on a cookie sheet as if it were a serving tray and set it on the ottoman. I thought maybe I would go to Target and get a real tray, and maybe a stand for him to eat on. And a handheld vacuum to pick up the crumbs.

Suddenly I wanted to go to Target right now.

"I'm going to shower," I told him. "Do you need anything else? I already told David you wouldn't be able to help him today."

He shook his head. "I'm great. I'm going to eat this, watch a movie, then to be honest probably fall asleep watching *Ellen*. But thank you for telling David."

"He's coming up to see you later, if that's okay. He wants you to tell him when would be a good time."

"Yes that's fine. I'll text him."

I rocked on my heels some more. "After my shower I'm going to run errands on the city bus. And visit my mom. Is this plan okay with you?"

"Yes. Thank you, Emmet."

I didn't hurry my shower, but everything felt off for me. It was almost lunchtime, but I hadn't eaten a proper breakfast yet, only cereal. My body was angry for not having real food. I needed to fix this situation before I did much else. I also needed to make a plan. The city bus came every twenty minutes, and we had a stop not far from The Roosevelt, but the more I thought the matter through, I realized I didn't want to ride it today. I also needed to see if my mother had time to meet with me later.

I flapped my hands, trying to shake off my agitation

from all the change. Then I gave up and texted my dad.

My parents both still work, but they can sometimes take time off to help me. My mom is a doctor and can't get away very well. My dad can stop and help me easier. Also, while my mom is the fixer, the one who helps with my problems, my dad is the calm one. Mom was who I needed to help with Jeremey, but Dad was who I needed now to help with me and my messed-up day.

He said he could take the afternoon off, and he came to The Roosevelt to pick me up just as David was coming up to say hello to Jeremey. We all stood in the hallway for a minute and chatted, or rather David and my dad talked while I stood to the side and waited for them to be done so I could get going. They didn't talk long, which I appreciated, and then it was me and my dad getting into his car and driving.

"Did you want to get lunch?" he asked. "Because I could sure use some B-Bops right now."

B-Bops is a local chain restaurant that is similar to McDonalds except so much better. They have fewer choices, but this is fine as I always eat the same thing anyway. Also, they are drive-through only. This means Dad and I eat in the car, which I enjoy since I can hum while I eat and no one will make fun of me. Dad never makes fun of me for anything.

The other thing I like about B-Bops is they have two kinds of drive-through, a driver's side and a passenger side. We always use the passenger-side pickup because it's fun to hand the worker the money and collect our bag of food and our drinks. Sometimes the people at the window know us and are nice to me, but Mom doesn't want us to go to B-Bops much, plus I don't live at home anymore so we rarely go out to eat together, so I didn't know anyone. But they were nice to me anyway.

At B-Bops I eat a pork tenderloin sandwich with no onion, fries, a chocolate shake, and a glass of water. Mom says this is the most unhealthy meal ever and should never be eaten. Dad says it's delicious and won't hurt us if we don't eat it all the time. He gets a quarter pound cheeseburger and fries and a large soda, though today he changed his order and got a chocolate shake too.

He didn't talk to me while we were eating, because he knows I don't like that. He let me focus on my food, which was tasty, and once we were done wiping our fingers and stuffing the wrappers into the bag, he began asking questions. "So what happened today to keep you off work? You said Jeremey wasn't doing well. Is he sick?"

"His depression is bad again." I rocked in my seat, staring at the dashboard. "It makes me scared and nervous. I want to go to Target and get trays so I can bring him food in the living room."

"Do you think the trays will help him be less depressed?"

At home, I'd been so sure getting trays would help. When he asked the question now, however, I wasn't sure anymore. "Maybe."

"Maybe they will help you help him more, which will be good for you. Helping and keeping yourself happy count as taking care of Jeremey."

I flapped my hands and hummed. "It makes me sad when Jeremey is sad."

"I know, sweetheart. That's what being in love does to you. You feel what they feel. The good parts and the bad parts."

I decided to tell my dad my secret. I was still nervous, but I needed someone on my side about this. "Dad, I want to get married to Jeremey."

All my insides felt jumbled and nervous while I waited for him to speak. My mom told me I have a brain octopus making it hard for me to focus, making it difficult to be like people on the mean, but right now the octopus was everywhere inside me. I needed my dad to not make fun of me for wanting to marry Jeremey. I needed him to tell me it was okay. I needed more too—I didn't know exactly what it was I needed him to say to me. I only knew that until he said it, I might barf up my pork tenderloin.

I couldn't read his face, which was no surprise, and I couldn't tell his emotion from his voice tone either. "I thought you might tell me you were ready to marry Jeremey. In fact, you took a little longer than I thought."

"Do you think it's a bad thing that I want to marry him? Do you think I shouldn't do it?"

He turned to look at me. "Of course I don't think such a thing. Even if I did, would it matter? You're an adult, Emmet. If you want to marry Jeremey, it's your business, not mine. But I'll support whatever decision you make. And for the record, I love Jeremey as much as I love you. I'm happy for you. I'm sorry if you thought I would have any other kind of reaction."

I felt slightly better, but not much. "I don't know how to take care of him, Dad. I don't think I can marry him until I can."

"That's not how marriage works, sweetheart. You learn how to help your partner as you go."

I knew he was wrong. Maybe he was right for marriages on the mean, but I knew to marry Jeremey, I had to learn how to care for him. Maybe what worried me, what I knew complicated matters, was that I had to learn how to marry his depression too. I could see the two versions, the Jeremey who smiled and laughed and made love to me, and the Jeremey who disappeared into darkness. I had to find a way to take care of them both, to show both parts of him my love.

I didn't know how to explain it to my dad, though. "Can we go to Target, please?"

He took me, and he didn't ask any more questions or sigh heavily the way my mother would have or keep arguing like my aunt Althea. That's my dad.

AT TARGET THE staff all greeted us as we passed them,

but a few winked at me and made me give them a high-five. This is because they'd all heard about the video and thought I was famous. Sometimes I'm tired of being famous, if it means I have to touch people every time I go to Target. Today I wasn't in the mood, and after two high-fives I gave my dad the sign for it to stop, and he moved between me and the workers and told them to give me some space, please.

It was nice, but sometimes I wish they would give me the space without me having to ask. I also wish I didn't have to have my dad ask for it for me.

I tried to imagine Jeremey's depression self as a separate person, a sort of shadow Jeremey. Not as an enemy Jeremey, but as another part of him. I saw him first as a gray shape, and then I imagined him as pixels, because I enjoy math. What did those pixels want? What did depression want? Technically what depression was or what it sought inside a brain wasn't known, but it was thought to be about neural circuitry. So it was similar to my brain octopus. But it was a sad octopus.

What did a sad octopus want?

I didn't know. I hummed and thought about it as I searched for TV stands and trays to bring food to Jeremey on. Target had some nice ones. I picked stands that matched our apartment but which were also sturdy (I had my dad check the construction) and I picked a yellow tray with a happy sun in the corner and a little monkey. It made me happy, and I hoped it would make

Jeremey happy too. Maybe Depression Jeremey would like it, maybe not.

I was coming around the aisle out of housewares when I saw the dog.

It was a large black dog with short hair, and it wore a blue vest with a harness. It sat near a man who was studying a shelf of light bulbs. The dog was pretty and well-behaved. I would have kept walking, only wondering why a dog was in Target because the man clearly wasn't blind so this wasn't a seeing-eye dog, but then I saw the words on the dog's vest.

Service dog.

I stopped and stared at the dog. Service dog? What service was it providing? My brain octopus went crazy, and I flapped my hands, because I had a feeling I had found exactly what I was looking for at Target, something more than food trays. I searched with my camera eyes for my dad, but he was still talking with a friend in another aisle. I wanted to ask the man about his dog. I flapped harder, trying to soothe my octopus so I could find the words, but I was so excited I couldn't calm down. I began to rock and hum as well as flap.

The man glanced at me, then quickly away. He tugged on the dog's leash and whispered, "Block."

The dog stood up, raised its ears, then moved between the man and me. When I took another step toward the man and his dog, the man gave another command. "Around." Now the dog traced big circles around the man, making it impossible for me to come closer.

I backed away because I had to—the dog kept making wider circles, and I either had to move or get knocked over, but I still needed to talk to the man. I wanted to look at him so I could tell him what I had to say was important, but he was nervous now too, gripping the dog's leash and acting as if he thought Target were full of enemies. I understood his feelings. I felt that way too. Except my enemy was his dog. I flapped at the dog and hummed, trying to tell it I needed it to stop, but the dog only made bigger and bigger circles, pushing me farther and farther from the man.

And then it led the man away.

I cried out and followed them, even though I was afraid.

My dad found me. "Emmet, what are you doing? Why are you chasing this man?"

I was so overwhelmed at this point I couldn't speak out loud. I yelped and frantically signed at him. *You have to stop him, I need to talk to him about that dog for Jeremey, please, Dad, please, please help me, Dad.* I kept signing until Dad ran forward and raised his hands in front of the man.

The man stopped, but the dog kept making circles and blocking us, and I put my hands over my ears and rocked, moaning. I was so afraid now, my octopus was trying to take my head off my body. But I didn't leave. I could see the man was listening to my dad.

Calm down, I kept telling the octopus. *Calm down, so you can talk to this man about this dog. Please, calm down.*

It was a long time before I got myself contained, but it took the man a long time too. We all had to move to the staff break room of the store, where the manager (who knew who I was because of the viral video and liked me a lot) brought us snacks and drinks. I didn't drink or eat anything, and neither did the man, but my dad had a coffee, and he and the manager chatted until the man who had the dog and I were ready to talk. They also brought me a green tea latte from Starbucks when I changed my mind and decided I wanted a drink after all.

Then my dad, the man, and I sat together at the table. The man told us his name was James, and he shared his story.

"Sorry for running away earlier. You startled me, and Lacie was protecting me. I'm a veteran, and I have PTSD."

I rocked in my chair. "That's Post-Traumatic Stress Disorder."

James nodded. "I upset easily, especially in public places. My brain has a difficult time understanding I'm not in a threatening environment anymore. Lacie helps me deal with things I perceive as threats. When you approached me and I wasn't expecting you, I got nervous, and so I had her block you, then remove me from the situation. Intellectually I knew you weren't a danger, but my brain doesn't listen to reason right now.

I'm sorry."

I wasn't upset about his inability to behave rationally, but I was frustrated because I had so much to say, and it was hard to get myself under control to speak. I knew I could say some of it, but I worried I'd start humming in the middle of words or shut down completely, so I decided to use my dad as an interpreter. I signed to him, and he translated, though he also added his own words, I noticed.

"Emmet isn't offended. He does want to know more about Lacie, however. His boyfriend has depression, and he wants to know if it's possible for service dogs to help with something like that as well."

James smiled. "Oh, yeah. A friend of mine, another vet, doesn't have PTSD so much as depression, and she has a service dog too. Her dog is her lifeline. Cassie fetches medicine for her, nudges her to take walks, monitors her for suicide, all kinds of stuff."

I was so excited I let out a kind of barking noise, which made Lacie perk up from the floor. Dad looked at me, and I took a deep breath, trying to push my octopus aside so I could use my own voice. "I want to get a dog for Jeremey. This is what he needs. A service dog. *Hmmmm.*"

"I can put you in touch with the people who got me my dog." James had his phone out and was thumbing through the touch screen. "It was a veteran's service, so they probably can't help your friend directly, but I bet they can get you headed in the right direction at least."

I flapped my hands while my dad got the number from James and thanked him for his help. Lacie watched me, and I watched her back, my octopus dancing inside me. I could see Depression Jeremey's pixels forming around the service dog, feeling her, deciding whether or not a dog would be okay.

Except I already knew the answer. I didn't need math to figure out this equation. I knew this would work.

I was positive it would. As positive as I was that $a^2 + b^2 = c^2$.

CHAPTER SIX

Jeremey

As New Year's Eve approached, I got the feeling Emmet was up to something, but I couldn't be sure.

My depression was intense, and as we've already established, it lies like crazy. It had plenty to say about my suspicion Emmet had something up his sleeve too, and all its whispers were terrifying, so I worked constantly to shut it down. There was also so much going on with the party preparations and getting ready for our houseguest. Icarus had approved Darren's overnight with us, and Emmet helped me make my room Darren friendly. Mostly this meant picking things up. Emmet is the reason my room doesn't dive into becoming a total trash heap, but my idea of tidy is still his idea of pretty screwed up, which is part of the reason I have my own room. Darren said he didn't mind the mess, but I'd roomed with Darren briefly and knew he appreciated neatness as much as Emmet, so I wanted to take the time to make the space he would borrow appealing to him.

Emmet helped, which I appreciated, as cleaning overwhelmed me, but he could only do so much because he worked. New Year's Eve was on Saturday night, but I had to do the cleaning during the week, and that's when Emmet had to be at work. So David helped me as well, as best as David could.

David is both my boss and my best friend. He's the first person I think to go to when I have a problem, outside of Emmet. Emmet and David are good friends too, though when they first met they didn't get along at all. We're the best of friends now. David used to tease me that he wished I could drive and then we could take on the world, but he knows it makes me feel bad, so he's stopped.

Technically I *can* drive, as in I have my license, but I get nervous when I do, and I've gotten more nervous as I've gotten older. I could maybe drive on a quiet street in a small town, but I don't think I could do Duff Avenue or Lincoln Way in Ames, the main in-town streets that most people from big cities would laugh at me for avoiding. Don't get me started on store parking lots.

To be honest, managing my own bedroom was struggle enough, but with David's help, I got it done. He could only do a little here and there with his grabber, but he redirected me and kept me on task, because as he put it, he was good at bossing people around. "Begin with the pile of clothes over there," he'd tell me, reminding me to sort them into piles of dirty and clean, and when it got to be too much, he suggested I call the whole lot dirty so we could keep moving. This was something Emmet would never have done. We'd have stood there for fifteen minutes having a discussion about each item. This was where David came in handy.

"You're making some good headway," he remarked after we'd worked for a half hour. "Why don't we stop and have a break?"

It seemed early to be taking a break, but I was exhausted. I wondered if it showed, then figured it probably did. Feeling glum, I nodded and followed David as he maneuvered his chair into the kitchen. I sank into a chair at the table before I realized as host and as his staff I should be the one getting our snack, but as I rose, he waved me into my seat.

"Sit. I got this." He snorted and gave me a wry smile. "Well, *maybe* I got this. Depends on how high up you put stuff and if I can reach it with my grabber." When I tried to stand up, he waved at me harder, his arm flapping awkwardly. "*Sit down*, Jer. It's a joke."

I didn't laugh. "Sorry. I've been…" I didn't know how to finish that sentence. Not without getting in trouble. *I've been a mess. I've been awful.*

"You're having a rough time. Which is why I'm helping you out." He snagged a box of crackers with his grabber and a stack of plastic glasses. "How's

Emmet doing since you confessed about the depression, by the way?"

"Intense. He wants to fix it."

"He wants to help you. Not the same thing."

"He can't see the difference." I watched David tuck the stack of glasses under his chin, pull on the stack with his more functional hand, managing to leave two under his chin. It was a neat trick. "Maybe he doesn't want to fix it exactly. He's up to something, though. It makes me nervous."

"No offense, but everything makes you nervous." He slid the extra cups onto the counter, caught them with his grabber, then aimed the stick at the cupboard. "Okay, I can get them put away, but they're not going in under Emmet's standards of neatness. I'll try to remember to explain to him, but if he gets bothered by this, blame me, you got it? It's the best I can do with my motor control."

"I'll tell him. It'll still bother him, but he'll understand."

"Cool. So what are we having? Water? Soda? Juice? Tea? Whiskey sours?"

The last comment was added to make me smile, and it worked. "There's green tea in the fridge. I'll have that please."

"Dude. If that's all there is, I'm having water." He opened the door, then exclaimed in excitement. "*Orange soda*. Are you for real?"

I'd forgotten about the soda. "It's for you. Emmet

got it the other day."

"*Train Man.* You come through for me."

David wrestled the containers out of the fridge with his better hand and the elbow of his not-so-good hand. This was a trick we'd learned together through trial and error. Apparently a physical therapist or two had also suggested something similar, he admitted later, but David and therapists had rocky relationships on the best of days. He and I, however, got along fine.

It took him about fifteen minutes longer to get us drinks and crackers and cheese than it would have me, but I didn't mind the time to sit quietly, and David, I knew, appreciated someone letting him do something for himself without trying to help or praising him afterward like he was a toddler. He said this was why I was a good aide, because I was patient. He told me I needed to remember, when the depression told me I was worth nothing, that I was the best aide he'd ever had.

I still didn't know how to explain to him it was like throwing a compliment into a black hole, so I usually replied, "Okay" and hoped he'd talk about something else.

Today he did talk about something else, thankfully. "Tell me about this Darren," he said around slurps of orange soda through his special straw, and bites of cracker and cheese. "He's autistic like Emmet, right?"

I thought about how to phrase my answer. "He's autistic, yes, but not like Emmet. He's nonverbal, to start."

"Like, he doesn't talk? At all? But I've heard him whispering to videos on his iPad."

"That's the only time he can talk, and that's as loud as he gets. Otherwise all he can do is make sound, but it's more like a bark." A thought occurred to me. "He's like Carly Fleishmann."

David sat up straighter, his whole demeanor becoming both serious and interested. David had a major crush on Carly Fleishmann, a young woman with autism and several other disabilities who had written a book with her father and become something of a minor social media celebrity. "Oh, okay. So does he use a keyboard to talk like she does?"

"Kind of. He uses a special sign language. Emmet knows it, but I haven't learned much beyond the basics. It's like ASL, but it's modified in ways that confuse me. Mostly he uses an iPad to talk for him. He's smart, but most people don't think he is. All they see him doing is watching YouTube videos."

"And you roomed with him at Icarus, right?"

I nodded, crumbling my cracker with my fingers. "Icarus is pretty grim. I wish we could get Darren into The Roosevelt."

David gestured at the walls. "Well, I told you about the opening. God knows there'll be more, and there's still nobody on the waitlist, not anymore."

"But that's just it. He can't afford it."

David's cheeks colored, like he was embarrassed.

He stared at his lap. "Oh. I…I could talk to my dad, if you want. Maybe…"

He didn't finish the thought, because he knew he couldn't get his dad to do anything like what Darren would need. Not with The Roosevelt already in trouble.

I laid the rest out, to make it clear. "Darren can't afford The Roosevelt, not in any way. He can't get a job. He's on disability, but his parents can't afford what it costs here. I mean, I couldn't do it without the discount from being your aide and Emmet's help with food and things. Which I feel bad about sometimes, but there's nothing I can do about it. It's expensive to live here." I realized what my remark sounded like and added, quickly, "Nothing against your dad or anything. I don't think he charges too much."

"No. I know what you mean. But that's the problem, apparently. It costs a lot to run a place like this, it costs a lot to live with disabilities, and nobody wants to pay for it. Nobody *can* pay for it, except the state, who won't." He rolled his eyes. "Too busy saving the money for the *normal* people."

Normal people.

I stood up and went to the window, folding my arms over my chest as I stared down at the street, at the sidewalk full of people coming and going. From school, from work. To friends, to family, to the grocery store. To the bus. Laughing, talking. None of them thinking at all about how high the curb was or how busy the crowd or how many strangers might talk to them.

Normal people. These were the people who deserved the money from the state, not me. What for, I didn't know. Tax relief, my dad would say.

They looked pretty relieved to me already.

Emmet would get after me for using the word normal, and I know he's right, but it's the word in my head. The people laughing on the street and not caring about anything while I was barely able to leave my apartment, barely able to get to the window to watch them—they were normal, and I was not. Emmet says they're *on the mean*, but this always sounds strange to me. What was the term, the usual term? Able-bodied, David said about people who weren't paralyzed. Technically I was able-bodied, by that standard, but I didn't feel very able. I'm not able to do a whole hell of a lot. I decided I wasn't able-bodied, because I was on disability, so no. The word wasn't for me either.

Able-bodied people didn't worry about things like I did. Like whether or not they could put themselves together enough to get through their day. Or a grocery store. Or a room cleaning. Able-bodied people didn't have to make a strategy to get things out of a cupboard. Or have a friend over. Or make sure they had a place to live. They didn't have to hope their parents kept paying their rent at their fancy residential facility. Or hope every time there was an election Congress didn't decide to cut their insurance.

Able-bodied people didn't look at history books and read about the populations sent to the gas chambers and know they would have been at the front of the line to be eliminated as unnecessary. Well, some of them did. Some of them like me had two strikes. Disabled and gay. If I were Jewish or Romany, I'd have three strikes.

I knew I wasn't wanted. Every day, every aspect of the world, of the culture, made a point to tell me I was different and less than, and so were all my friends. And I was tired of it.

I went back to my chair, tucked my feet onto the seat, and hugged my knees.

David came closer and studied my face like he was trying to read all my secrets. "Talk to me, J."

I shook my head, turning my face away. "If I talk, I'm going to say something awful."

David nudged my leg with his wheel. "Hit me with it. I want to hear your awful."

I swallowed, feeling guilty, but mostly…angry. "Sometimes I hate able-bodied people."

I'd expected him to laugh, even bitterly, or make another one of his jokes. But all I was met with was long silence, and when he finally spoke, all he said was, "Me too, Jer. Me too."

CHAPTER SEVEN

Emmet

I WANTED TO get Jeremey the service dog right away, before the New Year's Eve party. But I soon learned that service dogs were not easy to get.

I discovered there were different kinds of support dogs too, and they did different things. There were emotional support dogs, which weren't as expensive but weren't trained as well and weren't allowed into public spaces the same way James's dog had been. They worked with individuals, but they could just as easily work with any individual as the next one. They could be admitted to apartments that had "no pets" policies, but they couldn't do much else. Therapy dogs couldn't do that, and they also couldn't be brought into public establishments, but they could work with multiple people at once, which was more what they were designed to do.

What we wanted for Jeremey was a service dog. They were covered by the ADA, and the owner had the right to bring them into public establishments. They could tolerate a wide variety of experiences and environments. Like emotional-support dogs, they could be brought into apartments with "no pets" policies, but they were specifically trained to assist one person and were often tailored to meet their unique needs. This meant they were expensive.

Very expensive.

They required more time and effort as well. We were going to need Dr. North's help too, since a therapist would need to be involved in both the approval and the training, making sure the dog did what Jeremey needed it to do—but I soon learned, however, even if I had no financial issues, service dogs were still difficult to acquire. I found only one place in Iowa with service dogs, and they had a waitlist of six months. Also, they needed a deposit of five thousand dollars. I was glad I'd made the phone call with my dad because I couldn't speak after that. I began humming and flapping, and my dad had to get on the phone and finish the conversation with the woman I'd been talking to.

I didn't have five thousand dollars. I only had three thousand in my IRA account, and that was for retirement. And this five thousand dollars was only a deposit. They'd want more money later. Depending on the dog, I might need as much as twenty thousand dollars. It would be years before I could get a dog for Jeremey.

I hummed and rocked and flapped my hands, wishing I were at home in my apartment so I could go to my closet in my sensory sack.

"Hold on. *Hold on*." My dad was off the phone now, and he sat in front of me, using his *calm down, Emmet* voice. "That was our first call, and the woman told me there are places we can go for scholarships and grants, and other people in and around the Midwest training dogs we can talk to. The grants are competitive, and the need for dogs is higher than the availability, but here's where we might want to bring in our secret weapon. Because you know who is aces at writing grants and winning scholarships and bullying her way into getting what she wants for her kid."

Mom. He meant my mom. I flapped with a different kind of agitation now. *She's going to get bossy*, I signed.

"Probably so. Look, you take the good with the bad. Where do you want the bossy, son, helping your boyfriend get a service dog, or on the other side?"

I wanted bossy to help me without bossing *me*. Which wasn't possible. And I really wanted Jeremey to get the dog.

I thought he would tell her what was going on, but he didn't. He had me do it, which had to be in sign because I was worked up, so much so I made grunting noises like Darren while I told the story with my hands. I went to my apartment first to put on my Stitch T-shirt, which was my sign that what I wanted was especially important to me. I practiced what I wanted to say, writing it out and signing in front of a mirror, but even with rehearsal it was the most difficult thing I've ever done. I was quite upset toward the end. I had tears as I signed with angry and sloppy fingers. I don't know why Dad didn't just tell her. I was too worked up. And any second she was going to interrupt and tell me what to do.

Mom didn't do that, though. She listened quietly, and when I made barking noises—not like I was pretending to be a dog, they were part of my autism getting the better of me because my emotions were so over the top—she put her hand over her mouth. When I started crying, she started crying. I was a little upset, but I needed to finish, so I kept going until I was done, and then I signed, *I'm done*, and put my hands in my lap.

Mom sat there for a minute, not saying anything, keeping her hands over her face as tears leaked through her fingers. My dad stared at her, not crying, but he had one of those looks I can't read. Mom nodded at him and patted his leg. Then she turned to me. She didn't pat my leg, but she looked at me the way she did when I was ten and she promised she would take care of the teacher who had upset me and made me bang my head against the wall until I bled.

"Emmet, I will get Jeremey one of those dogs, as quickly as I can. And you will not spend one red cent, and neither will he, so don't worry about it, not anymore. Okay?"

I was surprised by this, but this *was* the same intense face, and she'd made the bad teacher go away the last time I'd seen it. I trusted her. *Okay*, I signed. Then, because it was polite, I added, *Thank you, Mom*. I remembered who had brought her here and added, *And Dad*.

Mom started crying again, but Dad only winked at me and rubbed her back.

We hugged also, and my mom called me her jujube many times, but eventually I went home and spent some time in my sensory sack.

When I came out, I still thought about the service dog a lot, but there wasn't much I could do about it, so I did my best to focus on other things, such as the preparations for New Year's Eve. We'd had parties before at The Roosevelt, and I knew how everything would go, the getting ready, so it was comforting to help. I showed up in the lounge, and Sally gave me a job. I was assigned to help prepare the snack food, which was a nice job because it was the same job Jeremey and David were already doing.

Jeremey smiled as he saw me come into the room. "Hi, Emmet. You're later getting home than I thought you'd be." He looked carefully at my eyes, and he put his concerned face on. "Is everything okay? Did something happen at your meeting?"

I knew he'd thought I had a work meeting when I was in fact talking about the service dog, but I didn't want to tell him yet, in case it didn't work. Though I realized now that I stood in front of him maybe I should talk to him about it before we got too serious. I rocked a moment, wondering if I should do it right now.

Jeremey put down the cup he was using to mix M&M's into the popcorn and approached me. He didn't touch me, but he came as close into my space as he could. As close as only Jeremey is allowed to get. "What's wrong?"

I shut my eyes for a long second and drew in a slow breath, letting the smell of Jeremey fill my senses. I would know him by his scent alone in the middle of a crowd of strangers. I know the perfume of him over his sweat, over the pollution of rooms he's walked through, of kitchens and cleansing agents and exhaust from cars. I know the color of Jeremey's smell—a bluish green with brown and white flecks and bits of yellow, like an ocean wave coming into my shore. I know the shape and geometry of Jeremey's smell, the weight of it. I have made computer programs to express how I feel about his smell, though I haven't shown anyone, even him, because I'm not sure he'd understand. I don't need him to understand, though. Not about the smell.

What I did need in this moment was for him not to worry, especially when there wasn't anything to worry about. His scent had calmed me, reminded me he was here and he was okay, that I was okay, that we all were. And I thought, there's no way Mom would get a dog tonight, so I could enjoy the party and find a way to tell

Jeremey about it the next day, or whenever it felt right.

I leaned in and kissed him on the cheek, my lips landing close to his, so I could feel the corner of his mouth under mine. I lingered there as I spoke, the scent of him rushing through me, making me wish we were alone because I would have had sex with him to show him I was okay. "I'm fine. I was emotional about something earlier, but it's all settled now. Don't worry. I'm happy to be here with you and David and everyone at the party." I kissed him again, this time on the lips, and I added, "I love you."

Jeremey leaned into me, putting a hand on my arm. He squeezed tight, a hard pressure so it didn't tickle my skin. "I love you too, Emmet."

DARREN ARRIVED AT The Roosevelt as we were finishing setting up for the party.

Sally went to get him, but it took her a long time, and when they came back, she had an angry face I didn't need any emotion flash cards to know what she was feeling. She smiled when she introduced Darren to everyone, but once this was done, she took Tammy's arm and pulled her into the kitchen. This meant they wanted to have a private conversation, but there was a window in the door, and I could see them through it. Tammy was raising her arms and pointing at the wall toward the street and yelling, but Sally looked angry too, so I didn't think Tammy was angry with her.

Something was definitely going on, but I couldn't tell what it was.

I wanted to ask Darren why they were so upset, as it was logical to assume he might know since he had been with Sally, but he was sitting on the couch watching a YouTube video and didn't look as if he wanted to talk right now. He had asked me for the WiFi password before he came over, so he was already hooked up and plugged in with his headphones. Probably he was nervous in a new space and needed the comfort of his videos before he could be social.

I decided not to ask him about anything yet, but I did think I should focus on making him feel welcome. Jeremey was busy helping David hand out snacks, and I didn't have a job assigned to me yet, so I assigned myself the job of keeping my friend company, because no one would know how to do it quite the way I could.

The first rule was you had to understand how much space he liked around him, especially when he was feeling uncertain about a new situation. No one else was sitting with him on the couch, but when I joined him, I made a point of sitting as far from him as I could get, and I didn't make eye contact or do anything to draw attention to myself. If you think about it, the whole sitting-down thing was pretty much attention-drawing enough. For Darren, me sitting would be like an elephant landing, though I was careful to disturb the couch as little as possible.

My autism makes me a highly sensitive person, but

compared to Darren my autism is nothing. I'm high functioning, and Darren is not. His autism keeps him trapped inside himself, and it has his whole life. There are people who think this is a bad thing, that there's something wrong with him and it needs to be fixed. Darren disagrees. He says the world needs to fix itself to accept him. He's not depressed at all, except he wishes sometimes he could find someone to share his life with. He isn't interested in body parts, but he is interested in romance. He flirts with people on Tumblr all the time, though it's Darren flirting so people don't always know they're being flirted with. He also gets in a lot of arguments there. I don't do Tumblr because there's not enough math.

Darren wasn't on Tumblr when I sat next to him. As I said, he was watching YouTube, which is what he usually does when other people are around, but also what he does when he's nervous. I could see from my camera eyes he was watching an unboxing video of someone opening Star Wars toys. He had the iPad close to his face, both hands on each side, his headphones tight on his ears, the hood to his sweatshirt pulled in close. He was tuning out the room.

I knew he could still see me, though, so I signed to him.

Hello, Darren. This is Emmet. Welcome to The Roosevelt. Do you want me to visit with you, or would you like to sit alone right now?

He didn't answer right away, but I waited, knowing

it might take him a minute to respond. Eventually he did, in Darren sign. *I would like to visit with you in half an hour. Would you mind sitting with me until then?*

I was fine with this, but I had to think a moment, because I wondered if Sally or Tammy would give me a job if they saw me sitting there. I decided what would happen was people would bother us. I knew how to fix that, but first I had to answer Darren. *I don't mind. Please let me know when you want to speak with me. I'll wait here until you're ready.*

Thank you. He went back to watching his video.

I pulled out my phone and typed a text to Jeremey.

Jeremey, this is Emmet. I am on the couch with Darren. We are visiting silently, but other people might bother us. Would you please bring me card stock and a marker so I can make us a do-not-disturb sign?

He answered right away. *Yes, I'll send David. Thanks for being a good host to Darren. I love you.*

A big ball of happiness expanded inside me, and I hummed and rocked. *I love you too.*

David came over with the supplies, and he looked as if he was going to say something, so I put my hand on the side of my face, which was my special signal for *don't talk to me*, and he said nothing, only handed me the stuff and left. He knew I didn't mean to be rude, which is why signals are so nice. After considering a moment, I put the card stock in my lap and wrote out the sign.

DO NOT DISTURB. SILENT CONVERSATION IN PROCESS.

Then I tented the sign and put it on the couch between us and waited.

I didn't mind waiting at all. I counted things, mostly, because I always find that soothing and relaxing, and
sometimes the information comes in handy. There
were fifteen people in the room and the adjoining
kitchenette, for example. Eleven men and four women.
Two staff, twelve residents, one guest. We had only
eleven places to sit, though, which would be a problem.
I texted Jeremey and told him this and suggested he tell
Sally to find us some more chairs, though of course
David didn't need one since he brought his with him. I
counted the ceiling tiles, though I already knew how
many there were, but I also counted how many people
were wearing blue, and how many people had shoes
with laces, and how many people were watching
television and how many were listening to the music. I
hadn't begun to run out of the kinds of things I
normally count, let alone had a chance to think of new
things, when I saw Darren sign at me.

I'm ready to talk to you.

I was glad to talk to him, but part of me was disappointed because I'd had fun counting. *I'm glad you could
come to our party. It will be fun to have you stay over at our
apartment. Did staff take your things upstairs already?*

*Yes. They let me in, and I put my bag by the door in your
foyer. I didn't look past the living room and kitchen, but your
place looks nice.*

It's a good apartment. Bob helped set it up so it would be perfect for the two of us. You should see my sensory closet.

Darren made a noise and rocked back and forth as he signed. *You're really lucky. The Roosevelt seems like a great place.*

Do you want to meet other people? Some of them are nonverbal, but some would like to say hello. Stuart screams a lot, so you might not want to meet him right now.

Maybe in a bit. I'm still kind of upset. There was an incident when I was leaving Icarus.

I wondered if this incident was why Tammy was still in the kitchen making hand gestures at Sally. *An incident with you?*

Darren hesitated. *Sort of. It's complicated. I'd rather not talk about it.*

Do you want to be by yourself in our apartment for a while? I could take you upstairs.

No. I want to be at the party. I'm trying to desensitize myself so I can participate.

This seemed reasonable. I've always admired this aspect of Darren's personality. *All right. I can continue to wait with you. Jeremey or David could join us too.*

Darren made another noise, this one like a seal, and he rocked hard, flapping his hands before he signed. *I don't want them to feel awkward because of me.*

They won't feel awkward. Remember. These are my special friends. They're the Blues Brothers.

Darren's mouth moved slightly, a subtle flicker of his lips. This, for Darren, was a smile. *They're The Roosevelt Blues Brothers. The best kind.*

Yes. And we want to be with you. Even if you're not at your best. We understand.

He hesitated a long time, then made the sign for yes. *Okay. If you think they don't mind. I can use my iPad to talk. I think I'm ready for that, with The Roosevelt Blues Brothers.*

I texted Jeremey, and he brought David over. David hadn't ever met Darren, I realized. We needed to introduce them.

I knew how to do introductions. I have several flash cards that help me practice them. I had them memorized, so I visualized them and tried to think of which one would be best to use right now with David and Darren.

"David and Darren," I began, once I'd selected an introduction card from my brain, "please allow me to introduce you to one another. Darren." I laid my hand flat and made it point to David though I'd just said Darren's name. This is because when I said Darren, it was to get his attention, and now I was going to tell him about David. "This is David Loris. He is the son of Bob Loris, who owns The Roosevelt. He is one of my best friends, and he is a Roosevelt Blues Brother." I hadn't ever called us Roosevelt Blues Brothers before, but I liked the way Darren had phrased that. I was going to use it from now on. I switched my hands and pointed to Darren instead. "David. This is Darren Kennedy. He is also my friend, who I know from when I lived in Iowa City. He lives in Icarus House and is visiting us this evening for the party. He isn't a Blues Brother, but he could be one. He should be."

David raised his good hand in an awkward salute as he smiled at Darren. "Pleasure to meet you, Darren."

Darren didn't look at David, but he lifted his iPad as it spoke for him. "It is nice to meet you, David. Thank you for having me at your party." He pulled the iPad down, rocking and humming as he poked at the screen. I waited because I knew he had something more to say, and soon enough, he raised the iPad. "I would like to be a Blues Brother. How do I apply for the job?"

I laughed and rocked, smiling at Darren's joke. He's a pretty funny guy. I've always enjoyed his sense of humor. David and Jeremey weren't laughing, though, and Jeremey appeared thoughtful. "I think we should consider Darren a Blues Brother, for sure."

Darren made another noise and shook his head. He signed at me, apparently tired of typing. I translated for him. "He says he has to be in a video first, to be a Blues Brother." He wasn't joking anymore, either, I didn't think. I signed back at him. *I don't think you have to be in a video to be a Blues Brother.*

David grinned. "I'm always down for another video. Been wanting to make one, actually. The question is, what song? It's going to be tough to top 'Happy.'"

Darren poked at his iPad. He rocked a lot, and he hissed through his teeth, which I knew was a noise he made when he got especially excited. He still made the noise when he held the iPad up to speak for him. "I will do research and find a good song and send it to Emmet to play for you. If you like it, I will help you make a new video. I'm good at tech."

"Oh yeah?" David leaned forward in his chair, as much as he could. "Say, *how* good are you? I see you have an iPad that helps you talk. I want to be able to do more on the computer, and my dad says he'll get me whatever system I want, but I'm overwhelmed with what to get. Do you know enough about that kind of thing to guide me through my accessibility options? Hardware and software, I'm talking."

Darren made a loud, excited sound, and he grinned at the top of the iPad as he typed. "Yes. I will be happy to help a Blues Brother out, anytime."

"*Sweet.* God, thanks, man. You think maybe you'd have time tomorrow? Unless I'm being pushy."

"I would like to help tomorrow. But it all depends on when I go back to Icarus." He typed some more. "If you get bored at the party, I would rather play with your computer than be in a room with strangers, to be honest. Say the word and we can go right now."

David perked up, then glanced at Jeremey and Emmet. "You guys mind?"

Jeremey looked at me, and I knew he wanted me to make the decision because he doesn't like decisions. I considered the question carefully. I wanted Darren to fit in with my friends, and I wanted David to get help with his computer. But I wanted to spend time with all of us at the party too. I decided there wasn't any reason we couldn't do both.

"Let's all go to David's room for a little while, but we have to finish in time for train dominoes."

"It's a deal." David backed his chair up, grinning. "Jeremey, steal us some popcorn on the way out, will you? Hell, load my tray up with all the goodies you want. Party's in my room, boys."

CHAPTER EIGHT

Jeremey

W ATCHING DAVID AND Darren work together was interesting.

At first I couldn't decide if I should help or not, because they each have physical limitations that don't exactly go together—David's paralysis and Darren's jerky mobility issues because of his autism. Something told me I should let them sort it out, though, and so I did. It took them a lot longer to get organized and settled at David's computer than if I had helped, but they managed it. David would have asked me if he needed assistance, and I trusted Darren would have done the same.

Soon they were engrossed in their work. Darren became excited when he discovered a cable that allowed him to hook his iPad into the back of David's system, and then he could use it to talk more easily to David as they worked. I'd forgotten how jarring it was to speak to Darren for long periods of time and hear the evidence of how brilliant he was, something it was easy to dismiss when glancing at his shuttered exterior. I'd never seen him like this, though, working with someone, helping them. All this intelligence was going to waste every day at Icarus, and it upset me.

I got out my phone and opened the notepad app so I could talk to Emmet without either of the others overhearing me.

I don't like that he's stuck at Icarus House on his own. It makes me sad to think of him there when I know he would be happy at The Roosevelt.

Emmet accepted the phone when I handed it to him. He typed a reply to me, but he also added initials and colons in front of our words because he needs things to have order.

E: I will look into my ideas for helping him more. I was distracted by another project, but I am free to pursue the Darren issue now. Though I worry I won't find any good answers. What he needs is a job. Money is a big problem.

I replied, adding my initial this time so I didn't upset Emmet. *J: Maybe he could help people with computers the way he's helping David. Maybe he could be an aide too.*

E: I don't think Bob could afford two aides.

This was true, especially given the shaky status of The Roosevelt itself. I hated money so much.

J: Maybe Darren could be David's aide and I could get another job. I didn't know what other job that would be, and the thought made me queasy, but I would find a way to get over myself if I had to, if it meant getting a place for Darren to stay.

E: You can't give up your job for Darren. Also, Darren isn't physically able to do what you do for David.

I hadn't thought of that. My shoulders slumped, and I leaned into Emmet as I typed. *J: I wish life weren't so hard all the time. It makes me so sad.*

Emmet held my hand and squeezed it. His squeezes are slightly awkward, but I like them because they're his. He surprised me by letting me go and turning to hold my face carefully in his hands and kiss my forehead before he took my phone. *E: Please don't let depression take away your party. Darren is having fun right now. You should have fun too.*

This was a good reminder, the kind of thing Dr. North would say to me. I nodded, then kissed his cheek and whispered, "Thank you," into his ear.

Emmet took the phone again.

E: I want to have sex with you later.

The request was a bit out of the blue, but that's how sex was sometimes with Emmet. He never missed a chance to plan it if he could. I blushed, thinking about sex with Darren next door.

J: We will have to be quiet.

E: You will have to be quiet. I am always quiet. You're the one who makes noise during sex. Do you want me to do research on what kinds of sex will keep you quieter?

I laughed, and he frowned, because he hadn't meant his comment to be funny, which made me laugh again. I kissed him on the mouth, and replied out loud this time. "No, I think I can handle it on my own."

We played Mexican train dominoes soon after, though Darren and David talked all the way down the hall, discussing software. David didn't mind that Darren's replies took time as he typed into his iPad, though while Darren and I arranged our seats at a table to play and I made space for David's chair, I heard David asking Emmet if maybe sometime he could teach David to at least understand some of Darren's sign language so he didn't have to type into the iPad. I smiled to myself, pleased to see the two of them were already so friendly. I liked how our group of friends was growing. Emmet was right. Darren would make a great Roosevelt Blues Brother.

Train dominoes went about the way it always did, which is to say it was fine for me and a blood sport for Emmet. There aren't any actual trains involved, only that you put your dominoes in a line *like* a train, but between the name and the math of it all, this was Emmet's favorite game in the world, and he played to win. Unfortunately so did Sally, who had also sat at our table, and I soon learned Darren wasn't holding back either.

David and I didn't exactly sit on our hands, but neither of us cared a whole lot about the game, not compared to the others. I think David would have been more into it if he could have moved his own pieces, but as it was he had to tell me which ones he wanted where and I had to place them for him. Some of them he was able to nudge forward, but laying them on the table was too delicate of work for his hands, and so the task fell to me. I didn't mind, but it was boring for him, when all he could do was tell me which tile to pick up and where to put it down. I didn't care much about where mine went, since if I did well, other people had to lose, and all I ever wanted was for other people to be happy and not upset with me. This drove Emmet a little crazy, but he was too focused on beating Darren to scold me for my poor play this time.

Darren won the game, which wasn't ideal for Emmet, but he's a good loser, and I think he was happy when he saw the prize for the winner: a pair of Bluetooth headphones. Darren hummed and hissed and hit the *thank you* button over and over on his iPad. They were nice headphones. I was glad Darren had won them too.

By this time it was almost midnight, so we turned on the television and watched the ball drop in Times Square. It was a time delay, of course, because midnight in New York had happened an hour ago. Though the party looked exciting, I could never in a million years go to anything as busy as that, but we had fun cheering and clapping at our party.

And then it was time for bed.

I gave Darren a tour of our apartment with Emmet, showing him where everything was, making sure he knew he was welcome to anything he needed. "I put fresh sheets on the bed, folded the way you like them. I remember how, I think, from when we were room-mates. If they aren't right, I know you'll fix them, but I tried to get them close."

Darren smiled, his nostrils flaring. He signed thank you—it was his kind of signing, which I don't know a lot of, but I knew the Darren thank-you sign.

"You're welcome." I gestured to the room. "I put towels on the bed too, for when you want to take a shower. Emmet will give you a tour of the bathroom, because he has more rules about how it should be used. But there aren't any rules about my room. I put all my things away so it wouldn't be cluttered. Emmet helped me autism-proof it, but if something bothers you, don't hesitate to tuck it into the closet or whatever you need to do. You know me. I'm not going to mind."

Darren stood still for a long second, no reaction, no movement. Then he signed, his gestures quick and jerky, his body rocking as he punctuated each hand flick with a soft moan.

He must have been speaking to Emmet, because Emmet answered in the same sign. He seemed a little flustered to me, but I didn't know why. Eventually he turned to me, his gaze fixed on my shoulder. "Darren would like to hug you. I told him it was okay so long as it wasn't a boyfriend hug."

I blinked, first at Emmet, then at Darren. *But Darren doesn't hug anyone,* I wanted to say, though of course I didn't. I only nodded. "Sure." Then I stood still while I waited to experience a Darren hug.

I tried to think if Darren had even *touched* me before, outside of accidental brushes of hands as we'd exchanged objects or passed each other in hallways. I couldn't think of any instance where that had happened. He was so touch averse, worse than Emmet. I wondered what I had said that had made him want to hug me, and why.

He approached me slowly, someone working up to a challenge. Darren was almost as tall as me, if he stood straight, which he normally didn't. Normally he didn't stand at all, preferring to sit on a couch or in a chair. Now he was before me, as if he were about to take me in his arms and lead me in a waltz, and I felt flustered. Darren was handsome, with dark hair and a pretty face, with sweet eyes. It was easy for people to not notice, to only see the external expressions of his disability, the way his body folded in on itself, the way it flattened him out and made him seem different than people on the mean. Right now, though, all I saw was a handsome young man, and I understood why Emmet had been unwilling to say yes.

Darren opened his arms and wrapped them around me like a vise. I couldn't hug him back, because my arms were trapped, pressed against my chest and rendered useless. His grip was rigid, controlling every element of the hug. If it were Emmet hugging me, or someone on the staff, or David, I'd have put my head on their chest and relaxed into the embrace. Something told me not to do this with Darren. It occurred to me his pinning my arms hadn't been an accident. For Darren hugging me meant just that, him hugging me and not the reverse. He could pin me, but not me him.

So this was a Darren hug. I'd never seen this before, let alone experienced it. I had a feeling few people had. I went soft inside, letting the privilege of my initiation sink in.

When he released me, he didn't look at me, but I smiled at him, biting at the side of my lip. "Thanks, Darren."

He made a thanks sign at me, and then he went into my room and closed the door.

Emmet hadn't shown him the bathroom, which I worried would be a problem. But Emmet took my hand and led me into our bedroom. Immediately he drew me into his arms, embracing me in his own kind of awkward, though the tension in his touch made me touch his face, kiss his cheek.

"Emmet, are you okay?"

His hands on my back gripped my shirt. "I don't enjoy seeing other guys hold you. Even if it's Darren, who I know only likes you as a friend. It makes me feel tight and scared inside."

Emmet was jealous. The thought made me melt into goo as I rushed to soothe him. "Oh, Emmet. I could never love anyone but you, ever. No matter who held me."

"I know, but it's not fun seeing other people touch you."

I nuzzled Emmet's jaw—carefully, so as not to stimulate his senses in a way that would make him uncomfortable. "You can touch me now. Wherever you want to."

"Take off your shirt, Jeremey."

I took it off, handing it to him when I was finished. He carried it to the hamper and tucked it neatly inside. "I'll wash it with my clothes and return it to you."

I didn't give a damn about my shirt, but I nodded. "Thank you."

Emmet stared at my neck, but I knew he was also looking at my entire torso, admiring it. Thinking of what he wanted to do to it. To me. I bit my lip, the same place I had when I'd smiled at Darren, except now I wasn't smiling, not at all. Now I was breathing long and slow, waiting for Emmet.

"Touch me," I whispered, when I couldn't wait any longer.

He put his hand in the center of my chest, splaying his fingers. I shut my eyes on a gasp and a breath, then opened them and watched as Emmet ran his fingers up and down, painting invisible lines across my skin with the pads of his fingers. My belly quavered, and eventually I had to clutch my fingers against the door to keep myself still for him.

"Is my touch too soft? Too hard?" he asked, fingers slowing to a halt at my belly button.

I shook my head, watching his hand. "It's all good. I like it. All the feelings."

"Do you want me to touch you more? Maybe without your pants?" His fingers tightened into a brief ball. "Maybe while I kiss you?"

"*Yes.*"

I tilted my face toward his mouth as he kissed me, moaning and canting my hips into his hand as he fumbled with my jeans. I had to help him with the jeans, and the kiss was clumsy because he was doing two things at once. Nobody's ever going to mistake our make-out sessions for porn shoots or movie moments. I don't care, though. He had his hand on my dick, and his mouth was on mine, and during the whole of it, I was in his arms, and he mine. I surrendered to the feel of him, the comfortable, safe space that was Emmet Washington.

When we stumbled to the bed finally, I only had my socks on, and I lay there watching, content and happy as Emmet undressed before he moved over me. He took our cocks together in his hand, brought mine in to help. Together we guided ourselves with a bit of lube toward release. Our breathing was heavy, bodies tight as we chased it—I shut my eyes and let go to the sensation of his body sliding against mine as we both fought for our orgasm. I listened to the sounds he made, the ones we made together, remembering, vaguely, the need to be quiet. Mostly, though, I spun out of my head, high on the feeling of being with the man I loved so much, until it was too much to bear and I cried out, my feelings and my ejaculate pouring out of me all at once. As I fell onto the bed, Emmet followed suit, coming onto my stomach, though he did so silently, with only a few gasps and soft grunts.

I lay there afterward, ready for sleep as he cleaned me up.

"Is it still okay if I sleep in here?" I could barely open my eyes, and my body felt like lead. I thought I should get the answer to this quickly. "I can go to the couch. It's okay."

"I want you to stay." Emmet finished wiping himself off, put his pajama bottoms on, and climbed into bed beside me. "I had an idea. I thought, if I feel like I need space, I could put pillows down the middle."

I smiled at him sleepily. "That's a good idea. We should get a big bolster, if it works. Then maybe we could sleep together more often."

Emmet pulled me to his body, tucking me close enough so my head rested on his shoulder. "Right now I want to hold you. Is that okay?"

I inhaled, long and slow, letting the scent of Emmet fill my nostrils as the weight of his body surrounded me, the thrill of the release he'd given me still humming inside of me. "Yes. It's absolutely okay."

CHAPTER NINE

Emmet

BY THE MIDDLE of January Mom still hadn't gotten the dog for Jeremey, which logically I understood was how this process went, but practically the situation was frustrating. Though Jeremey had good days as well as bad days, New Year's Eve being one of the better ones, he still struggled more than he should. He had another round of bad depression around the tenth of January, forcing him to stay first in bed and then in the apartment for several days, missing work and most activities.

I didn't take off work this time, though I wanted to. Jeremey insisted it would upset him more to think every time he had a bad round of depression I would get less work done, and so we'd reached a compromise. Darren came over to be my stand-in.

David stayed with him too, but there was only so much he could do, and Jeremey did need someone more able-bodied around him. Darren did have some physical limitations, but not as many as David, and between the two of them they could get a lot of nursing done for Jeremey when his depression kept him bedridden.

David had become close with Darren, so much so that I got jealous because I thought maybe David wanted to replace me as his favorite Blues Brother. David had said this idea was ridiculous, who could replace Elwood? But Darren helped him a lot, he told me, because he knew about software for people with disabilities, plus he understood David's situation. Also I stopped being jealous when I learned David had used his superpower, which was annoying people until they told him things they otherwise wouldn't tell anyone, and he'd super-powered Darren into confessing what had upset him on New Year's Eve. When I heard the secret David had discovered, I wanted Darren over to The Roosevelt as much as possible.

One of the problems with our population, autistic people and people with disabilities and depression and people not on the mean in general, is that everyone else doesn't care about us or think about us at all. Why this is a problem is because when able-bodied people on the mean don't think about you or care about you, when you need things, they don't listen. And people like Darren and David need a lot of things, more than people on the mean. I need a lot of things too, but I'm a different case because I'm high functioning. Plus I'm what my mom calls a poster child. I am not on a poster and I am not a child, but this means I am a good example, better than the usual, and this means people want to help me because I look and sound the way they think is right, the way people are supposed to be.

Who people don't want to help is Stuart, who yells all the time, even though he can't help it.

I have a difficult time with Stuart myself, to be honest. I know he can't help how he is, but his disability and mine don't always mesh well. It doesn't help that ever since the Roosevelt Blues Brothers made our video he's decided he and I should be best friends, which is something I don't want. I think he wants to be a Roosevelt Blues Brother too, and he's definitely not one. I feel bad saying it, but I could never be with him the way I am with David and Darren and Jeremey. He's too intense, too loud. He needs to be friends with Cameron, who is also loud and intense sometimes.

My reluctance to be with Stuart only proved my point, though. If Stuart didn't have family with money, he would be in big trouble because he would be somewhere like Icarus. There aren't many places in society for someone with disabilities such as his, and the places that weren't The Roosevelt are scary. Group homes like Icarus rely on public funds, and public funds are threatened because people in government decide we don't need it or are spending it badly. None of the people who decide these things go to Icarus and look at the residents. Or the walls with big cracks. They don't notice there are no pictures or all the rooms are sad-feeling, or all the games are broken. They don't talk to the staff, who are young and inexperienced and frustrated. They read reports by people who want to do other things with the money that is meant to be spent on our population, then make decisions convenient for their plans. My mom says they avoid looking too closely at us so they don't disturb their consciences. I think she's right.

The problem is, a lot happens when people don't regard you as a real person. They think they can ignore you, and worse, they think they can use you. Sometimes they think they can use you the way a staff member was using a resident on New Year's Eve, when Darren walked in and caught the staff member assaulting her.

He'd heard her crying out in her room, and though to most people it had sounded like the same kind of yelling as always, Darren knew the difference, and he went in because he thought she was hurt. When he saw what was happening to her, he started shouting too and turned on the alarm on his iPad. The staff member assaulting the resident had swung at him and tried to break his tablet. When the other staff had come, at first the assaulter had blamed the assault on Darren, but since they'd seen him in the lounge five minutes before, and since the female resident also accused the staff member, no one bought the lie. The staff member had been taken away by the police, and the resident to the hospital.

Darren had been offered a session with an emergency counselor and some anxiety medication, and given an extra dessert. This was all anyone had done to soothe him after what he'd seen.

This was why Sally was so upset, because she'd come into the middle of this mess and had seen how poorly the aftermath was being handled. Then she'd heard it was the fourth assault to have happened at Icarus in the past three years.

David wanted to get Darren out of Icarus, and in the meantime, he brought him over to The Roosevelt as often as he could. I think he told his dad, because Bob was always telling Darren to stay over whenever he wanted and had a funny look on his face that kind of matched the *guilty* emotion card in my deck, even though it made no sense because Bob hadn't done anything to be guilty about. Darren had stayed over three more times in our apartment, borrowing Jeremey's room. If it weren't for Jeremey's depression, I would have thought more seriously about taking him as our roommate for good and seeing if we could work out a deal for the rent. But when Jeremey's depression came back so strongly, he had to have his own space, and me mine. While Darren could visit, he couldn't stay with us all the time. It wouldn't be healthy for any of us.

Darren was great as a nurse, though, and he and David were perfect together with Jeremey. David always messed up the apartment when he was in it, knocking things over and leaving them out, but Darren went around behind him and picked them up, and he read all my labels and followed all the instructions because he knew they were important to me. I felt okay about leaving Jeremey when they were there with him.

It didn't mean I didn't think about Jeremey the entire time I was at Workiva, though, and I had a harder time with my job in general. Usually I'm a steady worker, and my supervisor tells me how much work I get done in a voice I know means she's impressed with how well I'm doing, but not in January. One day she called me into her office for a meeting, and she asked me if anything was wrong. "You seem distracted and unfocused, and that's not like you."

I had to rock for a minute before I could answer, but I didn't mind rocking in front of Kaya. She's kind and understands rocking and humming help me focus. She waited patiently while I figured out how to answer her question. "I'm fine, but I'm distracted by a lot of problems with my friends and my boyfriend, and with the residential facility where I live."

"I'm sorry to hear you're feeling down. Do you want to tell me about your problems? I would love to listen." When I didn't answer right away, she added, "We could go to the ball pit first, if that would help."

The ball pit was something Workiva had installed since I started working there, and I was proud of it because it was my idea. There are other companies that have stress-relieving things such as adult play areas, and a few have ball pits, but Workiva built the ball pit for me. Kaya says they're appreciative to have a brilliant worker like me in this area and want to do what they can to retain me. I can take my laptop and work in there if I want, but mostly I enjoy going in there and doing some thinking. It's like a sensory sack at work. Except sometimes other staff go in with me, and we play together.

Kaya went with me now, and we had fun jumping into the balls, throwing them into the air and at the walls. We never throw them at one another, but sometimes we play catch. Once we got done jumping around, we sat in opposite corners and tossed blue balls back and forth. I only wanted to toss blue balls today, and she said she didn't mind.

"Can you tell me what kind of problems your friends and Jeremey are having now?" she asked as we threw the balls.

I decided I could. "Jeremey is having bad depression again. He can barely do his job with David, and he isn't even watching *Ellen* much anymore. My mom is trying to get him a service dog, but it's expensive and takes a long time. I wanted to help, but it costs a lot of money. My friend Darren lives in a bad residential house. He wants to live in The Roosevelt, but it costs too much money and he doesn't have any, and his parents don't have much at all. I wish I could help him, but I think I'm going to have to pay for Jeremey to live at The Roosevelt soon. Which is fine because I want to marry him. But I don't know how his insurance will work if we get married. And I still can't afford a dog and his bill at The Roosevelt. And The Roosevelt is having trouble too because of the state budget changes and because of shady backroom deals." I squeezed the ball I was meant to throw tight in my hands, staring at it. "Do you think Workiva would pay me more if I worked harder? I could come to the ball pit less and eat my lunch faster. If I skipped my dessert, I could save five minutes. Also if I ate in the break room instead of the cafeteria, this would account for another five minutes. With ten minutes less ball pit time, that's twenty minutes a day. One hundred minutes a week. In a month I could save six more hours. Do you think Workiva would pay me more for that?"

Kaya was looking at me. It was a complicated expression, so I waited to see what she said, but it took a long time for her to talk. When she did, her voice sounded funny. "Why don't you let me talk to some people first and see what I can do without you having to give up your lunch or your ball pit time? We want you to relax and be productive, Emmet. You're an important part of our Workiva family. You help us a great deal, and we want to help you, and the people you love."

"They both need complicated things. I've thought about this a lot. I have done a great deal of math on the subject. I can show you my equations. The issue is quite complex."

"I don't doubt it." Kaya wiped at her eye. "Oh,

Emmet. There's nobody like you in the world. You're one of a kind, and I wouldn't have it any other way."

I didn't understand what she meant, so I nodded. "Okay."

"You told me your mother was working on the service dog problem? Would you mind if I spoke to her?"

I didn't mind, and I told her that. But she wasn't done. She said she wanted to talk to Bob too, and the staff at The Roosevelt, and Darren.

"I have an idea. I have several ideas, in fact, but I don't want to share them yet until I have more facts for you. I definitely want to help keep The Roosevelt solvent, though. I had no idea it was in trouble."

This seemed logical to me, so I told her it was fine, I didn't mind waiting. But I realized I might have accidentally told secrets. "I can't remember if I was supposed to tell you about The Roosevelt being in financial trouble or not."

"It's okay. I'll be discreet." She held up a blue ball. "Do you want to play some more?"

"Yes, please."

When I returned to my desk a half hour later, I felt much more relaxed the rest of the afternoon. This is because Kaya is a good manager and knows how to get her employees to do their work, and when they can't work, she doesn't shout at them, she figures out why they aren't working and helps get their troubles out of the way. She hadn't been able to remove my obstacles exactly, but she did make it seem less overwhelming, and it was enough.

I didn't think about the problem anymore through the rest of the workday, and it didn't bother me as much at home that night, either. I knew the issue was still there, but talking to her made me feel better, and I knew Kaya was good with ideas. I decided I would give her a day or two to come up with potential solutions, and in the meantime I would not worry about those subjects as much.

I found out she wasn't simply good at coming up with ideas. She was *great* at coming up with ideas.

"I DIDN'T WANT to tell you about it until I talked to my supervisor," Kaya told me as she came to my office the next week to give me the news. "But Workiva has a new outreach goal to do community service projects, and they've earmarked funding for those endeavors. Each team is responsible for making a goal, in fact, and you've brought me enough for our entire division. So I took my idea to the higher-ups, and they gave me the green light. I want to make The Roosevelt my project. In fact, that's what I want to call it. The Roosevelt Project. We're going to use the money to help your mom pad the grants she has and get Jeremey a dog, and Darren and David are going to help me help Bob make The Roosevelt more solvent. In fact, I if I can, I want to help *him* realize a dream he hasn't told any of you about because he's been so focused on keeping the doors open on the one building he already has. It turns out he never wanted to make only one Roosevelt. He always intended to take The Roosevelt statewide, to make other independent-living condominiums. The trouble, of course, is the private companies taking over from the state-run hospitals and group homes don't want to operate like he does. They want to make profits or break even, and his model requires more investment and less profit. He uses some pretty colorful language to describe what they're doing, but he's out of money and energy to make his model successful. I want to give him a boost of both, through this program."

It was a good idea. I still wasn't exactly sure how it all worked, though. "You mean Workiva will just give the money away to Jeremey and to Bob?"

"Yes and no. Workiva is a big company, with offices in more than Ames. When they do a project such as this, they get to count it as a tax write-off, which saves them money. But it also helps connect them to the community, and in the case of Darren, it might help find them a new worker. Maybe even David. They appreciate the kind of image this outreach gives them too, what it says about them. Meanwhile, Jeremey and David and Darren get jobs, Bob gets help for a project he loves. Everyone gets something in the end. It's a big trade."

"What types of jobs would they do, though? Ones similar to mine?" Darren and David were both smart, but they didn't have the degrees I did or understand tech like I did. Darren is good with computers and searches, but there's a difference between what he does and what I do. He could definitely learn my job, but it would take a lot more training. Would I have to do that?

She pulled up a chair. "Well, no, he wouldn't have a job like yours. Neither of them would, and Jeremey would continue to be David's aide. They'd be working on The Roosevelt Project with me and with Bob."

This made sense. I thought of the software David and Darren had come up with, the things they'd found that even David couldn't afford, that Workiva could. I flapped my hands. "Kaya, will Workiva get David special tools to help him work because of his disability?"

"Of course. We support our team members."

I laughed, and I didn't mind that it came out like a bark. "This is great news. When do we get to tell them?"

"I thought maybe we could tell them together."

I approved of this plan, except for one part. "Let's not tell Jeremey about the dog, not yet. Not until we have more information."

"Fair enough, though before any training begins, he'll have to know, because his therapist will have to be involved. How about I take you all out to dinner tomorrow night? I'll see if Bob can come too and explain The Roosevelt Project." She paused, considering. "Oh, though if you want the dog to be a surprise, I suppose I need to explain it without Jeremey there, so I might have to tell you before the dinner."

"I doubt Jeremey has the energy for a public dinner right now." A thought occurred to me. "Does this mean Darren could live in The Roosevelt now, since he'd have a job?"

"You'll have to ask Bob about that. And I should warn you, this will be grant money mostly, and special funding. It's not going to be as good as your salary. Not even close."

I understood what she was telling me, but I couldn't help hoping it would be enough money to get Darren into The Roosevelt, or that Bob would make a special exception for him anyway.

We ended up going to Aunt Maude's, a fancy restaurant not far from Wheatsfield. Technically we could have walked to it, but it was still pretty cold, so Bob took us in the special van David could drive his chair into, and Kaya met us there in her car. Jeremey did end up coming, which made me happy, though it meant Kaya would have to tell me more about the dog later. I was glad he felt well enough to leave the apartment.

Kaya had our table ready when we arrived, and she had an excited face on. She bounced when she walked and her smile was extra big.

"I'm so glad you could make it." She shook everyone's hands, though she only bowed to Darren, and he bowed back. Bob gave her a big hug, and then everyone sat down around the table.

I thought it would be Kaya who made the announcement, but it was Bob, and he started right away as soon as the waitress took our orders. "We called you guys here because Workiva has given The Roosevelt an offer, and I've accepted it. With Kaya as our coordinating supervisor, we're going to start something called The Roosevelt Project, an effort Workiva will help fund. We're going to try to not only make The Roosevelt more affordable and accessible to more residents, but we're going to find a way to make *more* places like The Roosevelt not only in Ames but in the whole state of Iowa. The thing is, though, we're going to need help. To start, we're going to need to go to the Ames City Council and get some backing from them, and the state level as well eventually. But we're also going to need manpower. This is where Workiva comes in. They're offering salaries for some entry-level organizing positions. It's part-time work, and it's on-the-job training. But I'll be there, and so will Kaya, and because it's his department, Emmet as well."

When Darren and David and Jeremey seemed confused, Kaya continued. "We want to offer you jobs, Darren and David. Jeremey, we know you already have your hands full as David's aide, though you of course would be accommodated on site as part of his team." She passed two binders to them, with big, easy-grip tabs and plastic inserts so they could turn the pages easier. "You can take your time reading the job descriptions, salary, and benefits packages. Unfortunately, not much is negotiable, but you're welcome to go to human resources and see what you can do. It's a little different because of the program we're using, but I don't want you to think you can't try."

Bob cleared his throat and spoke again as Darren and David stared at the notebooks. "Also, I wanted to add for Darren, as a perk of the project, housing is included. Now, we need to discuss it, because what I was thinking was having you room with David. Which, if you don't want to, David, we can consider another arrangement, but you've been telling me you didn't like living alone, and—"

"That's fine." David's voice broke as he looked up at Darren. "I'd be happy to share my room, if he doesn't mind. I mean, we'd need to make accommodations, set it up however Darren needed it. Dad would redesign the space. Right, Dad?"

Bob's voice was gruff when he spoke. "Right."

Darren didn't glance up. He didn't move at all, except after a long pause, he turned one of the pages in the folder in front of him. Then another. He drew a long, slow breath, then let it out. Then he signed.

Is this real?

I knew he was talking to me—I was the only one who knew his sign well enough to read that. I responded. *Yes. Kaya talked to me about it at work this week. It's all real. Not a joke.*

Darren's hands shook as he signed. *But this is my*

dream. This is everything I dreamed of. I'm afraid I'm sleeping.

You're not sleeping. This is a real thing.

He made a small noise, then rocked as he signed, *Wait, please.* He put his iPad on the table and typed, humming and rocking. Everyone at the table waited, glancing at one another as he typed. Then he hit play, and the computer's voice spoke for him.

"Thank you. Yes. I want to take this job and move into The Roosevelt and be David's roommate. Thank you to everyone for this. Thank you. Thank you."

Bob cleared his throat again, but his voice was still gruff when he spoke. "You're welcome, son."

Everyone wiped at their eyes, except for Darren, who kept rocking and humming softly. I didn't wipe my eyes either. But when Jeremey put his hand on my leg, then touched my hand, I took hold of his palm before he could give me the signal to ask if we could hold hands.

I knew he was going to ask. And I wanted to hold his hand too.

CHAPTER TEN

Jeremey

THE ROOSEVELT PROJECT getting started was such a wonderful thing. Darren was so happy being David's roommate, and they both loved their new jobs, though it was hard work for all three of us. I enjoyed going to Workiva too, helping David and everyone else begin the project which would, eventually, benefit so many other people. But if I were honest, I was worried, because there was suddenly a *lot* going on, and it was going to get worse.

Something else was coming, something more that Emmet and Kaya had planned, and it had something to do with me. The problem was, I couldn't begin to guess what this something might be. All through the first two weeks of February especially, Emmet had been strange, nervous, and excited, and when I asked him about it, all he'd say was he had a surprise for me and I had to wait. "You don't have to keep it if you don't want it," was all he would tell me, and then he would say, "but I hope you want it."

I got so nervous I talked to Dr. North about it, and this was when I discovered two things: I was right, something was going on…and *Dr. North was in on it too.*

"I don't want to tell you anything more without bringing Emmet in," he said, holding up his hands when I started to panic, "but we can certainly call an emergency session, if need be. I can assure you, however, that yes, Emmet has something he's been working on for you for quite some time, something he's quite proud of. It's something you will need to agree to, if you decide you want it, and it's not something you can say yes to just to be kind to his feelings, which I've taken pains to make him understand. However, I have a feeling this is a surprise you will welcome. And I agree with him, this is something that might well help you and your struggles with depression and anxiety a great deal."

This, frustratingly, was all he would tell me about it, except to say I wouldn't have to wait much longer for Emmet's planned reveal, and that he would happily call Emmet in and ask him to explain everything now if I so wished, because a stressful surprise was no kind of good surprise at all.

In the end I decided to trust Dr. North and Emmet and practice my AWARE strategy and sit with uneasy feelings. It turned out as Dr. North had said, too, because not long after we spoke, one day when we went to work, Kaya came into The Roosevelt Project workspace and announced we were all taking a trip together on Saturday. I could tell by the way Emmet reacted that this outing had something to do with my special surprise.

When I woke up on Saturday, I was feeling so anxious that I didn't want to go anywhere. I was tired, and the world was loud and overwhelming. It had snowed earlier in the week, then warmed up, and everything was slush and ice. Plus I was frustrated with myself, because lately it seemed as if everyone else was so excited with The Roosevelt Project...but I was the depression thorn in everyone's side, slowing the whole train down. Like everyone at The Roosevelt had gotten into a hot air balloon, but I was dead weight hanging over the side, keeping it from rising. So most of this week I had stayed home. It meant it was harder for David to do his work, but...well, it had to be better than having me there, messing things up. Pretty soon they'd find someone to help him, and they'd forget about me.

Right now, though, I had to go see Emmet's surprise, not wallow in self-pity. So I got showered, ate the breakfast Emmet put out for me, and let him lead me downstairs.

Emmet's parents were there, both Marietta and Doug, which I'd kind of expected, and Kaya, as well as Dr. North. Kaya winked at me as she held open the door to the van for me to get inside.

"Emmet, where are we going?" I asked as he sat

beside me on the bench seat in the far back.

He fastened his seat belt and began to rock, smiling to himself. "It's a surprise. But it will take a long time to get there." He held out his hand to me. "Don't be nervous. It's a good surprise."

I took his hand, and he squeezed it tight. Though he normally doesn't do extended touch, he held my hand all the way out of town, all the way to Des Moines, in fact.

We drove for hours. "Our destination is in southeastern Iowa," Marietta called from the front seat, smiling over her shoulder. "We should get there around late afternoon."

I understood that to mean they weren't going to tell me anything further about the destination itself. "Okay," I said, because there wasn't much else to say.

Kaya sat in the front bench seat with Dr. North. She winked at me, then leaned forward to talk to Marietta. "Hey, should we stop in Iowa City to eat lunch?"

"Oh, good idea." Marietta tapped her finger on her lip. "We should go to Trumpet Blossom. It's vegan, and it's almost entirely gluten free."

Emmet's mom had a thing about him eating gluten free, thinking it might be good for his autism. Dr. North seemed excited to eat there too, though, because I guess he's vegan too. I hadn't known that, but then, I'd never eaten lunch with him before.

We did end up eating at the Trumpet Blossom

Cafe, and I liked it a lot. It had a nice atmosphere, and the food was good, though it was a little different from what I normally ate. Doug bought us Dairy Queen for dessert after, which annoyed Marietta, but I said the chocolate malt I had really hit the spot, and she stopped scolding him. I worried if Dr. North would be offended because he was vegan and I was eating ice cream, but he only smiled at me.

Doug didn't only smile, he winked.

I was sleepy after the food, and when I started to doze as we got on the road once more, Emmet let me put my head on his lap and sleep. He petted my hair and my shoulder, soothing me.

"You can nap, if you want," he told me. "I'll tell you when we get to the surprise."

I love you, Emmet, I thought, but I was too tired to say it. So I squeezed his knee, then drifted off to sleep.

When I woke, we were at a farm.

It wasn't a typical kind of farm, but it was definitely a farm. I saw barns and tractors and sheds, and bales of hay and horses. But there were also lots of buildings, long ones, and some smaller ones that didn't appear to belong on usual farms. There was also a house, and a man and woman had come out of it to greet us. Marietta went up to them and shook their hands, and so did Kaya and Dr. North. Then they all came over to us.

The woman, middle-aged with weathered skin and a wide smile, put her hands on her hips and looked between Emmet and me. "Which one of you is Emmet? I want to meet the powerhouse who got this whole project started."

Emmet leaned forward, rocking in place. "I'm Emmet. But I don't know who you are."

She laughed. "Sorry about that." She stuck out her hand. "Sue Grant."

Emmet didn't accept her hand, but he relaxed, his rocking gentling. "Yes, I know you now. You're the owner and head trainer. I've sent you several emails."

"Yes you have indeed, and I've enjoyed them all." She withdrew her hand, not seeming upset that Emmet didn't take it, and turned to Jeremey. "You must be Jeremey, then. Are you ready to go meet your girl?"

I frowned at her. "I'm sorry. I'm Jeremey, yes, but I don't know what you mean."

"She's a surprise," Emmet told Sue, rocking more anxiously.

"Ah." Sue tucked her hands in her pockets. "Well, let's get you to your surprise, then, shall we?"

I still didn't understand what was going on, and I was unnerved to hear my surprise had a gender. What in the world had Emmet gotten me? I glanced at the pasture to my right, the one full of horses, and I shuddered. Oh, please no. I was afraid of horses. Besides, where in the world would I put one?

Sue and Emmet didn't lead me to the horses, though. They took me into the smaller building that was painted red with a large sliding door. When Sue opened it, I was hit with a strong smell that reminded me of the time I'd volunteered at the animal shelter. Then I heard the barking.

Dogs.

A rush of emotion I couldn't name went through me. *Did Emmet get me...a dog?*

Except as we walked down the hallway, I couldn't shake the feeling this wasn't a shelter. It was too neat, too clean, and there weren't enough dogs. I'd only seen three, and they were working with people. Staff members waved at us as we passed. The dogs in the rooms with them wore vests, and the animals were sitting like they were learning tricks.

What kind of shelter was this? Was this a breeding place instead? Something was up.

Then we came around the corner...and there she was.

The dog was a golden retriever, sitting on a mat in a room, wearing a red vest and looking right at me with the most beautiful brown eyes in the world. Sitting so still, so patient, as if she'd been waiting my whole life for me to show up, and now I was here and she was too.

My breath caught, and I squeezed Emmet's hand.

He squeezed back.

A trainer stood beside the dog. She smiled at me, crouching beside the animal. "Hello there. Are you Jeremey?"

I nodded at her, feeling like I was lost in a dream.

The trainer gestured to the retriever. "This is Mai. She has some training to do, but she's ready to meet you and get to know you today. Mai, go to Jeremey."

The dog stood, and with those brown eyes never leaving mine, she trotted over to me, sat, and looked up, waiting.

I stared at her, lost.

In love.

"Comfort Jeremey, Mai."

Mai stood, put her paws on my legs, then stroked gently against my chest, whining softly at me, begging me.

I melted, letting go of Emmet and falling into the dog's arms.

She covered me with dog kisses, loving licks on my face and neck, nuzzles complete with grunts that made my insides turn to goo. I hugged her close, wanting to cry and laugh at the same time. My whole body shook, reeling from shock and wonder and joy and fear, afraid to believe this might actually be the surprise they had brought me here to have. It couldn't be this, that we'd come all this way for a dog. Not for this beautiful dog, this wonderful animal, this perfect girl...might she be the secret Emmet had been keeping for me?

I ached all over, something primal in me wrapping around her, unwilling to let her go. This was what I wanted, what I hadn't known I wanted until right now.

But what if I was wrong, what if they were only showing me a dog, and now I was attached to something I couldn't have?

I had to ask. I couldn't get any more attached, couldn't let my heart break any more than it already would if I'd guessed wrong. "Is this...is she for me?" I whispered.

"Yes." Emmet stood behind me, not touching me but standing close. "She's a service dog. *Your* service dog. She's trained to help people with depression and anxiety. She can go with you anywhere in public. If you go to Target and you get overwhelmed, she can help you. If you're at Workiva and you need a break, she can help you get to a safe space. If you're at home alone and depression is bad, she can get you your medicine and a bottle of water, or the phone. She can stop you from hurting yourself. She can fetch someone to help you. She can comfort you when you need comforting and be your companion when no one else can be there."

I withdrew from Mai, looking at Emmet, too stunned for a long moment to say a word. "She...she can do all that?"

"Not *all*, not quite yet." Dr. North said this, coming closer to get a better look at Mai. "She's still learning, which is why she can't come home with you today. The staff here will work with her, and with you, and with me, to help her be the perfect service dog for you and you alone. Which is why it's so important for you to be on board with this decision, Jeremey. Right now she only knows basic commands. She's finishing her standard training, but when she's done, she'll have to start Jeremey training. Once she begins customizing to fit your needs, you have to be ready to commit to her and to the program."

I wanted to commit to her right now. Forever. I drew a deep breath to steady my voice. "When will she be done with her standard training?"

The handler smiled. "She's so close. Mai's such a good girl, working so hard, I bet she'll be ready by the end of the month."

I stroked Mai's ears, her neck, shutting my eyes when she nuzzled my face. "I didn't know this kind of dog existed."

"They're expensive," Emmet said. "This is why Workiva had to help. Mom found a grant, but Workiva had to help us finish. It takes a lot of money to train dogs like Mai. But I wanted to get one for you after I saw a man with one at Target. I've been trying to find one ever since, and now you can have one too, if you want one. If you want Mai."

"Oh, I want her." My heart felt as if it might explode, it was so full of love. "Thank you, Emmet. Thank you, Marietta, Doug, Dr. North, Kaya—everyone. I didn't...I had no idea you were doing anything like this."

Marietta came closer, crouched, and kissed his cheek. "You're part of our family. We'll do anything for you." She smiled at Mai. "She's beautiful. What a princess."

Emmet came around the other side, petting her in a more halting, Emmet way. "I wish she could come with us now."

"Once you're ready to make it official and the paperwork goes through, we'll bring her to The Roosevelt for some on-site training, even if her standard training isn't quite finished. Then she'll come back here and finish her lessons, and then she'll come home for good." The trainer smiled at me. "In the meantime, we have some training for you too. You need to learn how to use your new dog. She's a good worker, but you need to know how to tell her what to do. We'll help you figure it out. Are you ready to learn?"

I stroked Mai's neck. Stared into her sweet face, her eyes, thought about how she was my dog. *My* dog. Not only my dog, but my helper. My tool so I could do better at work and in every part of my life.

Would she make that much of a difference, I wondered? Would having Mai mean I could go to work with David more? Would having her on *my* team, as *my* aide mean I wouldn't be The Roosevelt Blues Brother left behind all the time?

I wasn't sure, not yet. But I did know when I looked into Mai's eyes, I didn't just feel love. I felt hope.

"I'm ready," I said, and let hope soar.

CHAPTER ELEVEN

Emmet

MAI CAME TO stay with us the second Tuesday in March. It was a nice day, sunny and bright outside, and three trains had gone by already. There was still some snow, but it was in clumps on the grass, none left on the pavement. It was warm enough Jeremey and David and Darren and I could wait outside for Mai.

Jeremey was practically flapping when the car with Mai pulled up and she came out with her trainer. Jeremey went to her, crouching to let Mai welcome and comfort him. The trainer had taught me some things too, and I thought it was interesting to learn how some of the things that looked like simple dog kisses and hugs were actually Mai's training. She'd been taught a lot of things specific to Jeremey: how to calm a panic attack, how to lead him away from too many people, how to get nosy people to stop bothering him, and how to lead Jeremey to The Roosevelt, or—my favorite—to me.

"Find Emmet" was a training module we'd spent several hours working on the weekend before, and we'd done training all over Ames. Mai is very smart—she can find me no matter where I hide, even if I'm quite a ways away. All she needs is my scent trail, and she can hunt me down. Another trick she can do is take a plastic booklet from Jeremey and flip to the right colored page, and there's my picture and phone number and Workiva information on it. So if Jeremey is at Target and has a panic attack and wants them to call me, he can tell Mai *get Emmet*, and she'll take the page to an associate and they'll know to call me. Mai is incredibly smart.

Jeremey loves Mai so much, and he barely knows her. He cried each time they took her away to go get more training after her home visits, and today he cried as she came to him, though this time she was home, never leaving him again. But this is how Jeremey is. He has a lot of emotions, and he cries them out. I don't mind.

We took Mai inside, and for the rest of the day we mostly stayed in the apartment and got to know her. I enjoyed having her around, but it was also strange. I was glad Jeremey had Mai, but it would take time to get used to having a dog around in my living space. I would have to vacuum more, I realized, and use more air freshener. Sometimes her breathing bothered me because it was loud. But she was also a beautiful dog, and she gave Jeremey so much happiness. It was nice to sit, all three of us on the couch, and be together like a family.

What surprised me the next morning was that I woke up and found a note from Jeremey saying he and Mai had gone on a walk. I was nervous about this because Jeremey doesn't usually do well on walks alone. But when he came back, he had red cheeks and ears and a big smile.

"I did it. I didn't run, but I walked all the way around Brookside Park. Even in the part on the trails. All by myself, with Mai."

I was proud of him. "Weren't you scared?"

"I was at first. But Mai was with me. When strangers talked to me and made me nervous, I gave her the signal they taught me to have her block strangers, and they left me alone. Except after a few times, I felt silly, because I realized no one meant to hurt me. So I stopped using the signal, and we simply had a nice walk, the two of us. But I knew I was safe. If I did need the signal, I had her."

I held up my hand for a high-five, and Jeremey gave me one. Then I held up my hand to Mai. "Good job, Mai."

She met my hand with her paw.

Jeremey started coming to work with us regularly now that he had Mai, and we were able to get more work done on The Roosevelt Project. We had important tasks to do now too. Then we met Linda

Weaver, and our goals for the project shifted yet again.

Linda was a state representative, and she came to us one day in March because she'd heard about our model for assisted living. "My sister has severe cerebral palsy. She's only forty, but she lives in a nursing home because we can't find anywhere else to give her the care she needs. She should be able to be among her peers or at least be more involved in society, but we can't find her a place. And yet Iowa is more interested in shutting down facilities than opening them. Meanwhile, here you are. What I love about The Roosevelt is so much of what you're doing is led by the residents themselves. Bob built this place inspired by you, David, but you're making it your own space. And now the four of you want to make more space for others like you. You're the leadership we need in this state. I want to do what I can to showcase you. Will you let me do that?"

She'd asked all of us, and she'd looked a lot at David, but everyone turned to me when she was finished, as if they expected me to answer.

I hummed and rocked, and signed to Darren. *Is she asking us to run for office?*

Darren rocked a few times before he replied. *I don't think so. I think she wants us to help her with a project to help her stay in office.*

Things began to make sense. *I think this is the poster-child concept at work.*

Possibly. We will need to ask her a number of questions. I have several I'm thinking of. I can write them down and you can ask them if you think she'll take you more seriously.

I hummed and shook my head before signing a reply. *No. If she doesn't take you seriously, I don't want to work with her.*

Darren smiles are sometimes difficult to catch, but I noticed that one. *Okay,* he said, and then he began to make his iPad talk.

It took a long time for him to type, and sometimes he skipped a word or two to save time so the sentence was not quite right and a little choppy. But Linda Weaver didn't seem to mind, and she was patient as she waited for Darren to ask his question.

"Why do you want help from us, when you're the one who's elected to a public office? Most of us haven't been through college."

Linda nodded at this. She smiled too, and it wasn't the usual look people gave Darren, the one that said they thought he was the R word. "It's a fair question. I'm asking you because, to be honest, I've been backed into a corner, and I need all the help I can get. I've talked to Bob and to Kaya, and I like the way you guys are approaching this issue. Plus I'm a big believer in having the people affected by the issues be represented in the issues. Much as I want there to be more persons with disabilities elected to office, there aren't many in the statehouse right now. I want young, aggressive people such as you to help stand up for people like my sister, who can't stand up for themselves. There's some bad legislation about to come through the committee

I'm on, worse than what we've seen already, if you can believe it. They want to award more contracts to private companies such as the ones that have made the mental health and nursing home situation so unbearable here in the state. They're going to make it harder for places like The Roosevelt to exist. I want to stop that bill. I want your help to do it."

My octopus got upset at the idea of more bad legislation happening, the *shit crick* getting thicker with more poop in it, but if Darren was upset, he managed his octopus well. All he did was type on his iPad until he could talk to Linda some more. "Will helping you get in the way of working on The Roosevelt Project with Bob and Workiva and Kaya?"

"Absolutely not. I'd make sure any efforts you made on my projects worked in tandem or were completely secondary." I thought maybe Linda was proud of Darren, or pleased. "Please ask me any other questions, any of you, as many as you have. I'm happy to sit here as long as you need me to."

She stayed with us a long time, answering Darren's questions. About the bill being proposed, who had sponsored it, and what the specific ramifications where. He asked other questions too, but my octopus needed a break for some of it and I had to count some things in the room, though I did hear the part where he asked her if she knew of any contacts who could make our job easier. Linda said yes, she did, and she promised to email them as soon as she was back in her office.

Kaya was at this meeting too, but she didn't say much, not until the end. She listened, letting Darren and Linda talk, sometimes taking notes. When it was over, she asked Darren if she could see him in her office.

"Am I in trouble?" he asked through his iPad.

She shook her head, not smiling exactly, but she had one of those unreadable expressions on, and it looked a bit like a smile. When the two of them disappeared, David laughed, one of his trickster laughs.

"She about shit herself through the whole meeting, her and the representative both, though I think Linda was more impressed than shocked." David's grin became wider. "People are always underestimating Darren. They all think he's some dummy, but then he lets out his smarts and they don't know what hit them. I bet you any money Kaya's offering him a real job. And he's not going to take it."

I didn't understand. "What do you mean, a real job? Darren has a real job. He's working with you on The Roosevelt Project."

"It's a grant-funded project. It doesn't have a long-term aspect to it, and he's still tied to Medicare for insurance. She's going to offer him something meatier at the company. But he'll say no, because he believes in this. You haven't heard the guy's sermons on how awful Icarus is and how he doesn't want anyone else to live anywhere else like it, ever. I get them every night, now that you've taught me how to read his DSL and he doesn't have to hammer at his keypad. The Roosevelt Project is the only job he ever wants. Darren is committed."

It turned out David was exactly right. Kaya did offer Darren a job at Workiva, and he did reject it for the exact reasons David mentioned. We sat together on the couch in my apartment that night after work while Jeremey and Mai went for a walk, and he signed passionately, rocking and grunting as he told me the whole story.

She wanted to give me a job in public relations, working with people online. It would have been a good job, and maybe I should have taken it. But I can't now that we're working on this project. I believe in The Roosevelt. I want to make it a real thing. I want to do what Linda Weaver said, except I want to make it a project for the whole country and the whole world. I don't want anyone to ever feel like I did at Icarus ever again. I don't know if we can make the project that big, but I'm not going to take a different job when I could maybe have a job where I was part of that change. It's not what a Roosevelt Blues Brother would do.

This made me smile. I signed the Blues Brother sign to him, and he signed it back to me. It's something we invented, Darren and me: two shakes, fist closed, then a fist bump together. Our secret code, our badge of honor.

We still need to make a new video, he added. *I've been thinking of songs. But they have to be part of our campaign.*

We kept working on the project, with Linda Weaver and on our own, writing our grants and setting up our proposals. We were scheduled to go before the Ames City Council, and we all rehearsed our part in our presentation. Jeremey and Mai were doing great too. I thought maybe when the meeting was over it might be a good time to make plans to ask Jeremey to marry me. I thought maybe once we were done with all the proposals I could make one of my own. We were big time Roosevelt Blues Brothers now, and everything was going to be amazing.

Or rather it would have been amazing, if it hadn't been for RJ King.

RJ KING'S FULL name was Ronald Jeremiah, which I knew because I Googled him, but he kept introducing himself only as RJ King, smiling at everyone and making them laugh. This was the first thing I noticed about RJ King, that he was good at getting people to like him, better than David or even my mom. He only sought out people in suits, especially men, and he tried to make them laugh. Also, RJ King didn't wear a suit. He wore a cream sweater with three subtle patterns on it with a light-blue button-down beneath it, a pair of tan slacks, and a flashy gold watch that kept catching the light and making Darren jump in his chair.

Darren didn't like him. I could tell from the video he watched on his iPad.

"RJ King. Executive Director, King Enterprises. A pleasure to meet you, sir." He invited people to lunch, though some people he only offered to buy drinks. A few people he offered to take to the first football game in the fall, but he told everyone they should go golfing with him.

Whoever RJ King was, he cared about making friends with people in the room. I wondered if it worked. From the way everyone smiled at him, it seemed as if it might. I didn't want to take that many people to lunch or to games because it sounded expensive and exhausting, but I told my brain to remember the strategy for later to see if I could revise it to an Emmet version.

When the meeting came to order, we all sat down, including RJ King, though he sat in front next to several people Kaya had told us were important. She'd explained the meeting to us, how a long part of it would be boring and we'd have to sit through it, but I wasn't concerned. I sat through boring meetings all the time at Workiva. I knew how to listen and count at the same time.

The meeting was boring, but RJ King smiled the whole time as if it were the most exciting thing he'd ever heard. I listened harder, trying to decide what I was missing, but no, it was still boring. Though I supposed I hadn't thought much about the way my city worked, all the things that went into government. I realized there were law books and city codes I could read and I would understand the rules of Ames better, and I made a note to look them up.

Finally we came to the part of the meeting where we were allowed to speak. Kaya went first, which was part of the plan. Kaya smiled as she went to the microphone in the center of the room, positioned so the ring of council members could see. She wore a pantsuit because she said it's what powerful women she admired wore when they were serious about things.

"Good morning." She nodded at the council. "I'm Kaya Kovanen, representing Workiva, who is sponsoring The Roosevelt Project. As you know, Workiva believes strongly in investing in the community, and through several of our employees whom you'll hear from shortly, we believe this project is one of the best ways we can give back. I've provided a dossier for each of you detailing how we've already invested in this project and where we intend to invest in the future regardless of what the council decides. Please don't hesitate to ask me any questions today or in the future. But for now, let me turn the presentation over to the real brains of the operation, our Roosevelt Project team members: Emmet Washington, David Loris, Jeremey Samson, and Darren Kennedy."

Kaya mentioned my name first because The Roosevelt Blues Brothers had taken a vote and they'd decided I was the leader and should do the talking. I thought it should be David since he was Mr. Charmer and had better voice modulation than me. This had become an argument quickly, and in the end it was Darren who solved it.

"Each one of us has a disability that will make able-bodied people biased against us. There's no point in selecting someone to speak for us based on which disability is most pleasing to the able-bodied people, and anyway trying to please them is counter to what we stand for. I vote for Emmet as our representative because this was his idea in the first place, and he's the smartest. Plus he has a way of convincing people to do things they don't want to do. I think this approach could be good."

I didn't think I convinced people to do things, but the others had all agreed with him, and so I was voted leader. Now here I was in my suit and tie, my hair nicely combed and all my social cards memorized as I crossed the room to where Kaya stood at the podium.

I told myself not to be nervous, but the octopus on my brain could never stay calm in front of all these strange people. I'd given presentations before, and I had some tricks I'd developed with Dr. North, but this was a unique situation. Of course, so were the circumstances that brought me here, and this was what I'd decided to use to feed the octopus today.

I know this is scary, I told it. *But we need to get the council to listen so we can get the funds to help The Roosevelt Project get started, so I need you to rock yourself today. I will spend as much time in the sensory sack as you need later. Right now I need to convince these people I'm a leader. Work with me, octopus.*

I know I don't actually have an octopus in my head, that this is a metaphor my mom helped me imagine when I was little to help me visualize my autism. But sometimes, such as now, when I spoke to my octopus, I could feel the tentacles stroking the sides of my face, as if it were telling me it understood. I knew I would be okay, that I would do a good job.

As I crossed the room, I made a point to look at each one of the council members and smile, nodding. I'm aware I don't do this gesture quite right, that I'm too deliberate, but I've calculated it's less awkward to appear incorrect than to seem standoffish and not acknowledge people at all. Once I'd done this, I acknowledged Kaya too and stood at the podium, placing my hands on the wooden surface. Kaya had told me I could use the podium for notecards, but I had memorized my speech, so I didn't need cards. I did, however, need somewhere to put my hands so I didn't flap. I did plan to rock, but I'd practiced and I would do it subtly, mostly pushing back and forth with my hands. Only people on the sides would notice I was swaying, and they weren't the council members.

"Thank you for having me." I paused, smiling as I found an interesting pattern in the wall above the mayor's head to focus on. "My name is Emmet Washington. I work on the Data Science team at Workiva, and I'm a liaison at The Roosevelt Project. Additionally, I'm a resident of The Roosevelt. I graduated from Iowa State with a double major in computer science and applied physics, but despite several offers from companies around the country I chose to remain in

Ames because I wanted to remain near my family and my partner, Jeremey Samson, who is also a member of The Roosevelt Project and a resident of The Roosevelt."

I paused, because we had all agreed a pause was right here in my speech. This is the thing about giving presentations. You have to have pauses and know your timing. It's tricky. And don't get me started about vocal intonations. But I designed a computer program to help me map the proper places for rise and fall, and once I memorized my technique, I was fine. I think I probably still sound somewhat artificial, but I'm a Roosevelt Blues Brother, so I'm hoping it comes off cool.

"I was attracted to Workiva because of the company and its work, but mostly I wanted to remain in Ames and live at The Roosevelt, and this was the company that allowed me to continue to do that with the best situation possible for me. What Bob Loris created is a unique and wonderful living environment for me and others such as me. It offers us a chance to not only be independent but to have agency in our lives. We aren't second-class citizens shut away and forgotten, not at The Roosevelt. We are contributing members of this city, this state, this country. We hold jobs, participate in our community, and live our lives."

It was time for another brief pause, and I used the moment to check the council members with my camera eyes. My octopus rocked happily, and I let myself hum softly under my breath. Yes, everything seemed to be going well. Which was good, because now it was time to deliver the part Darren had written, which, as my mom would say, had a knife in it. This means the words are pointed and direct, not that I am going to cut anyone.

"The problem is The Roosevelt is costly to run and expensive to live in. The vision I've painted for you just now is pleasant and ideal, but it's a privilege only the wealthy can afford. Those in our community who need this kind of residential care but don't have the means are being increasingly left out in the cold, and unlike those of us fortunate enough to be able to afford The Roosevelt, they *are* being treated as second-class citizens, particularly in light of decisions being made by the state legislature regarding closures of mental health institutions and bills being moved through committee that would award more contracts to private companies instead of allowing the state to run the facilities as it has in the past. While it's true private companies are picking up the role the state was playing, by no means are any of them stepping forward at the level of The Roosevelt, not with any kind of quality of care. Abuse and neglect are increasing at public and private facilities, facts that members of our project team can personally attest to.

"The Roosevelt Project's mission is simple: we wish to be a bridge between public and private efforts to offer residential care to communities like ours. We want to offer safe, positive, affirming living spaces in Iowa for adults, new adults in particular, who need extra assistance in their daily life. We want to help funnel both government and private funds to offset the cost so this kind of assisted living need not only be available to those who can hold down jobs or those whose families have enough income to afford the care throughout their lives. We want to encourage business models that mean there are few to none of these toxic, poorly managed companies promoting alienation and abuse."

This time when I paused, I could tell I had the council's attention. Some of them were interested and maybe excited and others were probably agitated. I couldn't read faces well, not without looking directly at them and not while trying to contain my octopus, and anyway, I had to finish up. Thankfully I was nearly done.

I nodded at David, and as I continued to speak, he rolled forward. Jeremey came with him, and they worked together to hand out portfolio packets we'd prepared for each council member.

"In the proposals being provided to you now, you'll find outlined a detailed prospectus of cost, analysis, and goals for our project. The request for the City of Ames is highlighted in yellow, but you'll see also lines where we'll be requesting money from the state as well. We will also continue to solicit funding from companies like Workiva and other private donors. The information for our charitable organization is in the back of the binder. We're happy to answer any questions you might have, either today or in the future."

This was the end of my speech, and I waited patiently while the council members flipped through the proposals David and Jeremey handed out to them. I rocked in place with my hands, which wasn't always the most subtle of a rock, I have to admit. It had been a big speech, and my octopus was getting a bit out of hand. When the mayor leaned into her microphone and smiled at me, though, my octopus calmed enough to let me listen to her.

"Thank you, Mr. Washington. That was quite a testimony, and this is an impressive packet of material. I look forward to reviewing it in more depth when we're out of session. While you're all clearly motivated and capable, you haven't run charitable organizations before. Do you feel you're prepared to do this cause the justice it deserves?"

I wasn't quite sure what she was asking, and my octopus began to get nervous. I glanced at David and made the sign against my cheek for him to take over. He came to the podium, though of course he couldn't stand at it the way I did.

That bothered me. There should be a podium for people in wheelchairs too.

David motioned for Jeremey to hand him the mic, and he began speaking as if he'd planned all along to answer questions now, though Jeremey had to hold the microphone in place for him because his hand didn't want to cooperate. "You're right, we don't have the kind of experience you reference, and no, we don't intend to do this ourselves. You'll see in the documents in front of you we have plenty of outside help, largely through connections my father has. But you're talking with the four of us because we're the heart of the program. We're who we want you to see."

Now I understood what she'd asked. I motioned for the microphone, and Jeremey passed it to me. "We want you to see not only the four of us and our passion and motivation but also our disabilities. We want you to see our autism and our quadriplegia and anxiety and depression and all the things that mean we need places like The Roosevelt. We want you to see me standing here trying not to flap my hands or rock, trying to modulate my voice and make eye contact and do all the things you find normal, doing all kinds of things to make you feel comfortable. To understand how difficult it is for us."

I pointed at myself. "When I finish talking to you, what you think was such a good job will cost me so much I'll have to go home to my apartment and zip myself into a bag in my closet and hum until the sensory overload goes down. I don't mind, because this is important. But this is why I spoke instead of Kaya or one of the lawyers or the people who run the charity with more experience. They are all able-bodied. I am not. *We* are not. But because people in our lives have cared enough about us to help us, we've been able to do incredible things. What we are asking is why not care enough about more people in Ames so they can do more incredible things?"

"Or even everyday things." David spoke without the microphone, but he didn't need it. "Able-bodied people aren't expected to do superhuman feats each time they walk out the door. It should be enough to simply exist. We could start with ending abuse and neglect and giving everyone a more level playing field. We shouldn't have to tell you we want to cure cancer to get a few extra bucks. We should be able to say we just want to be able to ride the bus like the other citizens in the city. To enjoy life the way everyone else takes for granted."

This was true. I hummed quietly before lifting the microphone. "Yes. It's about the same chance as everyone else. The Roosevelt didn't get me a job or a boyfriend or any opportunity. It only helped me achieve my goals. The same as the privilege of able-bodied people does every day. This is all we're asking for: a leveling of that privilege."

Kaya had moved into the line of my camera sight, and she made our private sign for *Emmet, stop talking now*, so I stopped talking. The council regarded each other, a few of them whispering. I couldn't read their faces, but David seemed happy, so I decided it was good.

But as I said. RJ King was there.

As the council whispered, he stood, slowly. When the mayor saw him standing and asked if he had a comment or question, RJ King held his hand out to Jeremey. "Would you pass me the microphone, son?"

I didn't like the way RJ called Jeremey son. I didn't like how he called himself initials, or that his real name was so similar to Jeremey's, as if he'd stolen it somehow, but I didn't want to think of him as King or Mr. King either, because then it was as if I'd crowned him emperor of Ames or something. Except King was better than RJ or anything else, so it was what I went with.

Jeremey passed King the microphone, walking over to him and handing it to him. King held out his hand, smiling at the council now, and they smiled back at him.

"Well, that was certainly a wonderful speech, and before I say anything else, I want to thank these boys for coming out and standing up for such a worthwhile cause. Well done, gentlemen." He winked at all of us, then turned to the council, his expression changing to something more serious. "Having said this, I want to caution the city against rash involvement in such ventures as these young men are proposing, however well-intentioned."

A man stood up from the seat beside King, holding a stack of folios similar to ours but with better folders and design. He passed them out to the council members as King kept speaking. "Inside this document you'll see King Enterprises' research on how much the The Roosevelt Project would cost long term, and as you'll note, the drain on the city is substantial."

Kaya stood too, walking to the man passing out folios. "I'll take one of those, thank you." She snatched one from the man and flipped through it. Her face became complicated. I couldn't tell if she was angry or scared or both. "Where is your documentation for this?"

"The appendix." King smiled at her, and I decided I hated his smile.

"We want to see one of those too, please." David had been the one to ask for the document, but when the assistant handing out folders gave him one, he passed it to me instead.

I examined the notes, wishing I could hum to get rid of some of my nerves, letting myself rock slightly in place as it was impossible to stand there and do nothing. There were a lot of facts and figures in the document, a lot of tables meaning nothing, so I went right to the appendices. At first they upset me quite a bit. I worried King was right, there was no way The Roosevelt Project would ever be able to turn a profit for anyone.

Then I looked more closely at the numbers in front of me, and I began to hum.

As Kaya and King argued and the mayor tried to bring order to the meeting, I let the octopus out, let it curl its tentacles around the edges of my mind. *The numbers are wrong,* it kept telling me, and I knew it was right. I didn't know how yet, and if people would stop yelling, I could find it, but I knew they wouldn't stop yelling. I needed my sensory sack, my own space, but I couldn't have it, not right now.

Jeremey came up beside me, not touching me but sitting on the other side of me, coming close enough to block out some of the bad feelings from the front of the room. Soon David closed in on the other side, pushing a chair away to roll his into place.

"You found something, didn't you?" David didn't whisper, but he kept his voice low.

I nodded, still rocking. "It's too loud in here."

Jeremey touched my leg briefly. "Do you want to leave?"

I shook my head. "We can't. If we leave, he wins. I need to find his bad math while we're here in the room. Before the meeting ends. But I can't get my brain octopus to behave."

Darren appeared in front of me, blocking out the last line of sight of the meeting. He signed to me. *Let us be your sensory sack. We're your Blues Brothers shield. Tell your octopus it's safe with us. See if that helps, and try again.*

I wasn't sure this plan would work, but it was worth a try. I shut my eyes and let the octopus out, told it what Darren had said. I could still feel Darren and David and Jeremey around me, and I let the octopus feel them too. *We're safe with them. Let me be calm here so I can work out this problem and save The Roosevelt, please.*

I waited to see what the octopus would do.

It didn't move right away, but it did move. It didn't believe that The Roosevelt Blues Brothers were the same as a sensory sack. But the octopus liked the Blues Brothers, and it did trust them, and after a minute or so, I felt it calm down.

You can work now, it told me.

Letting out a breath, I checked the numbers once more.

With my octopus off my brain, I found what was bothering me in ten minutes. The discrepancy wasn't a mistake, not technically, but the information King had given wasn't accurate, and it was enough that I knew it wasn't right to present things the way he was. I started to explain it to David, but I didn't get far before he stopped me, had Jeremey get the microphone from the mayor, and then I was at the podium again, no more Roosevelt Blues Brothers buffer, rocking my octopus as I tried to explain what I had seen.

"The appendices Mr. King uses are quite thorough, and his math is technically accurate. However, I disagree with the way he figures his calculations. As you can see on page twenty-five, paragraph three, he uses a low estimate at a critical place, an estimate so low it is almost an error. This is acceptable as a hypothetical option for the projection of one outcome for the project, but to offer this as a singular vision is narrow-minded and a departure from reason. To use this low figure in this formula at this juncture affects all the other totals and implies the project is never viable, which is not the case if you use a median estimate. But this isn't the only place where they use a low estimate, either. Throughout their program it's clear they use low estimates whenever possible, thereby skewing their results."

King laughed, but the sound was loud and sharp and made me jump. "I assure you, there's nothing wrong with our projections. It's natural for you to be upset, young man, when the facts prove you can't get what you want, but this doesn't give you the right to stand up here and invent fictions. You couldn't possibly look at those complicated reports and understand anything to the degree you're talking about."

"There are a number of things wrong with your projections. I have my laptop with me and can show you, though it will take me about a half an hour to write the program, and I'm not sure the council wants to keep the meeting going while I do that, so I might have to bring the program to you after. And I *can* read complicated reports and understand them. It took me longer than normal because it's so loud in here, but I was able to see how the calculations were put together. It's only math. Math isn't complicated. It's only numbers and calculations. I love math. I'm exceptional at it. I'm good at assessing data too. It's my job at Workiva. It's what I do all day long." I stared at the folder, because I didn't want to look at King or the council anymore, not even with my camera eyes. "As I said, it would be one thing if this were one projection beside a more median-based formula. The best arrangement would be three lines, a conservative line such as this one, a median line representing an average, and a positive line representing an ideal. This is in fact a very good formula. I've memorized it now and could use it produce the median and positive lines for you by this evening, though I would rather give it to you tomorrow so I could spend tonight in my sensory sack and with my boyfriend. It's been a long day."

King laughed. "You *memorized* the algorithm we used to make those calculations? By reading it? Be serious. You're taking the game too far."

Out of the corner of my eye, Darren signed, *Tell it to them. Show them your brain. Tell them the formula.*

I thought his request was strange, because they wouldn't understand the formula at all, and I couldn't possibly show them my brain, that would be disgusting, but Darren is smarter about these kinds of things than me, so I told them the formula King Enterprises uses, reciting it out loud until Kaya stopped me, explained most people didn't know what those symbols meant, and would I please use the marker board, so I did. I didn't care for the way people were looking at me, because they had strange expressions on their faces, but once I was at the marker board it was easier. My octopus got nervous, but I reminded it The Roosevelt Blues Brothers were with me, and it didn't go crazy.

When I finished, I felt as if I'd run for miles. I was

tired and my arms felt heavy. I wanted to go home. I wanted my sensory sack. I wanted to sit on my couch with Jeremey and Mai and listen to trains. I didn't want to ever go to a city council meeting again. But it seemed it had been a good thing to do, though it exhausted me.

The mayor was staring at me, but I could tell the expression on her face meant *impressed*. "I believe the council has some investigating to do on this matter before we make any decisions. But, Mr. Washington, yes, I'd be interested in seeing those median and positive lines, whenever you have the leisure to produce them."

I couldn't speak. I was so tired. I found Jeremey's hand and squeezed it hard.

Jeremey squeezed back, and he spoke to the mayor for me. "We'll get them to you as soon as we can. Thank you."

I looked at Kaya, who was smiling at me like nobody had ever smiled at me before. But I also looked at RJ King, who wasn't smiling at all.

I had won this battle, I knew. But I had also made myself an enemy, and I had a feeling the next time I met him I would need more than math to take him down.

CHAPTER TWELVE

Jeremey

L IVING WITH MAI was a whole new life for me. We still worked on training all the time, but from the first day we were together, she changed everything. It sounds so strange, but the simplest, most important thing was I was never alone anymore. I hadn't thought about how much peace of mind she would give me until she was a part of my daily routine, and in fact it wasn't until the trainer came to visit me for the two-week checkup that I realized how much was different with her around.

So much of having a service dog was mindset. I was braver, even without her fully trained. I could face stores on busy days and navigate congested downtown festivals full of well-meaning people who overwhelmed me. Most of the time Mai didn't have to do anything at all. Simply being present was enough for both me and the other people around us. She made other people aware something was going on, alerted them they should behave differently around us, which was what I'd wanted all along.

Sometimes, though, people ignored her service dog vest and decided they should come over and introduce themselves to her, which always got awkward. Kids were pretty easy because Mai didn't hesitate to knock them over if they stayed too close during the *around* command, and whatever parent or guardian was with them ushered them quickly away. Adults who wanted to approach Mai while she was working, however, were a more complicated problem. They never took her hints when she blocked them or used *around* to make space for me. Adults usually began to scold me if I failed to engage with them or didn't let them engage with her, at which point I would have an anxiety attack and Mai would have to remove me from the scene.

Things were different, however, in April when the four of us went to the art festival and a rude person approached Mai, and the others were with me.

It was a street festival, most of Main Street closed off so we could wander between the booths, with a few food trucks at each end. A couple of the restaurants had tables stationed here and there as well, the fancy Thai restaurant and the co-op, as well as two of the downtown pizza places. What I wanted was hot chocolate from the Café Diem stand, so the four of us were trying to weave our way through the crush of people.

David led us because he was convinced people got

out of the way for wheelchairs once they noticed him, and he always made sure they noticed him when he wanted to get through. It was working, mostly, but the crowd was thick and full of people making too much noise. I was starting to change my mind about the hot chocolate. I couldn't imagine it'd be worth all this trouble. Except I was chilly, and I wanted something sweet and warm to hold on to while we walked around.

Mai noticed I was uncomfortable and moved closer to me, whining and pawing my leg in a manner meaning I was to pet her head and release some of my stress, to remind myself she was with me and I didn't have to face the crowd alone. I did as she asked, and the gesture worked as it was supposed to. Except a middle-aged woman with frizzy gray hair bent over with a big smile, leaning in too close as she came in to pet Mai.

"Oh, she's a *sweetheart*. Is she a purebred retriever?"

The calm Mai's command had brought me vanished, and panic rushed in as I realized how this encounter was going to go, especially when I ignored the woman and gave Mai the *around* command. The woman looked both astonished and affronted, puffing up for a lecture.

Before she could so much as open her mouth to start, though, Emmet appeared. "Mai is a service dog. She's wearing a vest that says *service dog* and *do not pet* on it."

The woman became more flustered than ever, tipping her chin up. "Well, I didn't see it. He could have said so and not had the dog push me away."

David had stopped plowing through the people and turned his chair around, wheeling up beside Emmet, Darren flanking him. "Mai is a certified service animal, and Jeremey has social anxiety. Your interrupting and not paying attention to his dog is putting him at risk of having to give up this event and go home. He still might have to, all because you thought you needed to pet his dog. I know what you're going to say. You didn't mean any harm. Well, here's the thing. You don't have to mean any harm to still cause it. So the next time you see a dog you want to pet, check for a vest, and ask for permission. If you don't get it, don't take it." He spun his wheels sharply in a move he liked to do when he wanted to appear aggressive, placing his chair a foot or so closer to her. "Now, if we could go back to enjoying our day, that'd be great. Thanks."

The woman sputtered as she hurried away. I watched her go, not sure if I was going to be leaving too, or what. Mostly I was stunned. What had just happened?

My gaze slid to the others, who were all watching me. Well, David was looking at me, but Darren and Emmet had their gazes fixed on things near enough to me I knew they had me in their camera vision. As I looked at Darren, though, his eyes flicked briefly to me, and he grinned widely as he held up his iPad.

"The Roosevelt Blues Brothers to the rescue," the robotic voice said.

I couldn't help a smile, though I still felt rattled. Mai nuzzled my leg, and I crouched to rub her head. This time she nuzzled my face and neck, giving me doggy kisses, and I shut my eyes and let her give them to me. This was one of the things we had begun to train Mai for specifically for me: to give me touch. I would never have thought to have a dog touch me, and it was odd at first, almost wrong, because all I could think of was I was substituting Emmet's distaste for too much touch with a dog's touch, and that didn't seem right at all.

But there was something different about the way Mai nuzzled me, something different than the way anyone else touched me. Her love was so unconditional. She was a service dog, yes, so she was working, but she was so sweet. I felt like she truly loved being with me, that we had bonded and she *wanted* to be my dog. I certainly wanted to be her owner. I loved taking care of her, loved getting her food and putting out her water and keeping her area clean. Taking her on walks never bothered me, not even if the weather was unpleasant. And I noticed simply taking care of her helped keep my depression at bay.

Mai was a Roosevelt Blues Brother too.

I ended up not having to go home. In fact, I didn't have an anxiety attack at all. I did need to wait with Emmet in a quiet place while Darren and David got our drinks, but this wasn't bad either, because I got to sit with Emmet and enjoy the nice afternoon.

"Have you seen any art you want to buy?" I hadn't had time to look around, but I knew he'd have been checking out things with his camera vision.

"There are some pieces I want to investigate more closely before we leave. They might be nice in my office at work." He touched my leg, a firm pressure, briefly. "Are you feeling better now?"

I nodded and returned his touch with the same kind of pressure. "Yes. Thank you for helping me with the woman. I didn't know what to say to her."

"There's not much for you to say on your own. This is where we're a good fit, the two of us. I'm blunt and it gets rid of people."

My heart swelled with love for him. "Can I lean on your shoulder?"

"Yes."

I put my head carefully against him, knowing how firmly I could press so it wouldn't be too soft or too hard. I enjoyed knowing I was the only person who could navigate his personal space like that. "Did you give the city council those formulas, or whatever you call them?"

"The projections? Yes. I gave them to Kaya, but we went to City Hall together, and the mayor took us to lunch. I think she was angry with RJ King for trying to deceive her. Kaya says we'll probably get the funding."

"Oh, good! Now all we have to do is repeat the same steps at the state level."

"I've been thinking, and I have a bad feeling about

it. I think RJ King didn't like how I beat him by finding his math formula. I don't think we'll be able to find his next trick so easily."

"And you think there'll be a trick for sure?"

"Yes. He doesn't want there to be a Roosevelt at all. Not our building and not a Project. If we succeed, Kaya says, we're a threat to him, because he's one of the biggest investors of the companies the law would give the funding too. But it's going to be difficult to beat him at the statehouse. He's friends with a lot of the legislators and the governor too. He calls the governor *buddy* and the governor smiles at him and pats him on the back. I found a video of it on YouTube."

I didn't fully understand what Emmet was talking about, but I could tell it was serious. "We need to have a meeting with Kaya."

"Yes. But I think maybe we need to have a Roosevelt Blues Brothers meeting first." He rocked on the bench, his gaze darting to the place where we had argued with the woman who wanted to pet Mai. "I think we need to have a lot of plans if we want to win against King. More than a computer formula."

Darren and David appeared around the corner, David talking animatedly to a silent Darren as he balanced a tray full of hot drinks, and casually flirted with women who stared too long at his chair. I stroked Mai's head and smiled at them, my heart filling with warmth. "I have a feeling we can make as many plans as you need."

CHAPTER THIRTEEN

Emmet

*W*E NEED A NEW VIDEO.

This is what Darren said when we sat down to make our first draft of ideas for plans. David had to go to physical therapy, and Jeremey and Mai went with him, so Darren and I sat at my kitchen table in our apartment to come up with some initial ideas.

I rocked in my chair and hummed as I considered his suggestion. I enjoyed doing viral videos, but I couldn't see how doing one would help us convince state legislators to give us funding for our project, so I told him this. Darren had his keyboard with him, hooked up to his iPad, and he typed as furiously as his fingers would let him so his computer could speak for him.

"You need to get the people on our side because the people are the ones who control the legislators. King will control the legislators with money and other kinds of influence we don't have. The only control we can afford is that of the people. So let's control them. If we make a viral video that sells our idea and introduces us to everyone in the state or maybe people outside of Iowa, then we win public opinion. When King tries to get people to vote against us, King and his legislators look bad."

While I understood the concept behind his reasoning, I felt it was based on nebulous reasoning. "We can't be assured people will contact their legislators simply because they enjoyed our video."

He signed this time. *No, but it's a start. It certainly can't hurt.*

He had a point. I hummed some more while I considered. "Okay, but I think we need a two-pronged approach then. We have the viral video *and* we try to do something else at the same time, something more practical. I think we should identify key representatives and make our case to them one by one."

Sounds good.

"The problem is I don't know how to identify them."

Darren grinned and made his barking, happy noise before he signed again. *You leave it to me. Now you're talking online research and information gathering from social media, and that's my area. You keep focusing on numbers.*

There weren't any numbers to focus on right now, but I decided I would find some because they'd be soothing. "What song are we going to do?"

Darren rocked and hummed, and I joined him as

we considered. Every so often he would play a song on Spotify, and we would listen to it before discarding it as an option, though there were a few we liked well enough for him to put into a playlist we called the Viral Maybe list. The problem was neither one of us was good at this sort of thing, and though we had seventeen songs by the time David and Jeremey returned, we didn't love any of them, and when David took a look at our list, he didn't love any of them either.

"I'm down with the idea of the viral vid, though. I've been itching to do another one of those since forever. Let me think about it for a bit, and I'll get back to you, okay?"

Except David didn't come up with anything. There were songs we all thought were good, but nothing fit our theme for The Roosevelt Project and what we were trying to do.

"It's got to be something selling the idea of helping people grow." David scrolled through his music library. "Something about hope and the future and trying new things and having your own life…fuck, there's no song like that."

We kept searching, though, until one day we found it. Or rather, Jeremey found it.

He'd gone to Walmart with Tammy, which was crazy because he hated Walmart, but he was looking for a new dog bed for Mai, and he didn't care for the ones anywhere else, and someone had said there were some soft ones for not much money on special at Walmart.

Jeremey came home with a dog bed, but he also came home with a song title, something he'd heard playing on the overhead speakers while he shopped. The song was "Try Everything" by Shakira, from the *Zootopia* soundtrack.

None of us had seen the movie, so we all watched it together. It was a nice film about not judging people by appearances, though I had a difficult time accepting some of the creative physics of the cartoon animals.

Of course since we watched it in the lounge, the rest of The Roosevelt watched it too, including Stuart. Tammy had suggested we watch it there since everyone else would enjoy it, and she'd rented the movie on The Roosevelt's money, so I couldn't say no. I wish I had bought the movie myself so we could have gone to my apartment. I couldn't hear half the movie because Stuart kept making noises. He insisted on sitting next to us too, trying to get my attention. He was always bothering me lately, always touching my arm and making noise at me. Sally told me Stuart considered me a hero, that it was flattering, but to me it was annoying.

The song Jeremey found was pretty much everything David had wanted in a song. The singer talked about how she wanted to try everything, wanted to do it all, though she knew she would fail, and she would keep trying and fill her heart with love, wouldn't give up or give in. It had a nice beat, and we could all see how we could dance or move to it, even Darren who would have limited movements.

I like this song a lot, Darren signed.

David nodded. "There's a lot to it, but it's not so nailed down it can't be stretched to fit our message. I remember it now from when the movie was out, but it's not so overdone we can't use it. Plus it's been awhile, so we're reviving it."

I imagined us dancing in our Blues Brothers outfits to it, and I couldn't help smiling. "Where would we film the video? Not Target again."

David shook his head. "No. We take this baby on the road. We do some on the Internet on our own, but then we go places where other people will take video and do the job for us. We get Mai a Blues Brothers outfit to go under her service dog vest. Or something so she's part of it too. Emmet, I say we get Kaya involved at this point. She's going to have ideas."

Kaya did have ideas. She was a big fan of our "Happy" viral video, and when she heard our plans for "Try Everything" and David's thoughts for a statewide tour, she made high-pitched noises and bounced up and down. "*Yes*. Oh my God, *yes*. I'm going to talk to marketing, but I have *so many ideas*. You guys are going to have to tell me what you can and can't do, but I think we could make this work. Both promotional for The Roosevelt Project but also advance work to undercut King and his cronies." She looked as if she wanted to hug me, and she almost did, then ended up hugging herself instead. "Sorry. You're making me too excited."

I smiled at her and held up my hand. "Let's do this instead. High-fives."

She gave me a high-five, but then she started to cry, which I didn't understand. She said she was happy, not sad, but I went to my desk to do math, because my octopus had had enough Kaya for a while after that.

WE BEGAN PRACTICING for our new lip sync the same day we decided on the song, but I could tell right away it was going to be different than when we did "Happy" at Target.

I suppose it made sense because "Happy" was a celebration for Jeremey and for the three of us, but "Try Everything" wasn't a celebration. We had an agenda, as Kaya kept reminding us. We weren't setting up the song to have fun. We wanted to convince people to call their representatives and support our project. Or be willing to call them later. It was complicated to put the message into a dance move.

"Don't think too much about making sure your dance achieves the right result," Kaya told me when I expressed my concern. "Your job is to convey the right *message.*"

"But the right message is the one that achieves the goal," I pointed out.

She said I should have faith, but I had never liked this answer, so I kept trying to use math and algorithms to solve the gap between our message and the goal. It didn't work, though, no matter what I did. I researched everything I could, but the more I investigated, the more I discovered this was a place where prediction could not win.

I warned you, Darren said over chat when I finally asked him for help and he confessed he had nothing to give me. *If there was a way to harness public opinion, political scientists and the entertainment industry would do it. Sometimes they manage to find a way, but it only works for a while. Human brains don't want to be controlled.*

I don't want to control them. I only want to explain to them why our way is the better way.

But even as I typed to Darren, I realized I *did* want to control their brains. Not for long, and not for a bad reason. But if I had to control them to get The Roosevelt Project settled...

I thought of RJ King and his algorithm that tricked the city council. I wondered what else he would think of to control the state legislature, how he was controlling the voters. Did it mean I should try to control them too?

Did I have to be like RJ King to beat RJ King?

My head began to hurt, and I said goodbye to Darren and put my monitor to sleep, but when rocking in my chair didn't help, I got up to go to my closet and my sensory sack. Except for the first time ever I didn't want my sack. Or my bed, or my hammer, or anything. I didn't know what I wanted. I was confused, and lost, and overwhelmed.

I wandered around the apartment, humming, pacing along the edge of the carpet where it meets the hardwood floor. My octopus was wild, and I wanted to pound my skull against the wall to stop it. All the sounds were too loud, the scrape of the clock hands in the bathroom, the roar of the refrigerator, the banging of the water as it dripped into the sink, the loud echoes of air rushing through the furnace, and water burbling in the pipes.

A song and dance could never beat RJ King. It would take lies and tricks and algorithms. Was I not smart enough to lie and trick the way he did? Or not mean enough?

Why did it feel as if I could see the future, that I already had the algorithm in my hand and it was telling me the good guys would lose and the bad guys would win, that the math was stacked against me?

Footsteps in the hall startled me out of my thoughts, each thump on the floor echoing in my head. I twitched when a key clawed at the lock, and I wanted to leave, to go to my room and hide, but I couldn't. I knew it was Jeremey on the other side of the door. I heard him speaking softly to Mai, in his loving voice he only uses to her, telling her they would go inside and get a treat and then sit and watch TV together. Jeremey talks to Mai all the time, and hugs her. She is his sensory sack, except he can have his sensory sack on a leash and use it almost anytime.

I didn't want my sensory sack right now, though.

Or, at least, I didn't want the one in my closet.

My head hurt so much, pounding on the top right side of my skull, making my eyes water. The room felt too bright, too sharp, and I wanted to leave it, but what I wanted more was to see Jeremey. I didn't know why. Part of me was afraid when he and Mai entered the room the stimulus would be too much and I would have a breakdown and embarrass myself and upset Jeremey and not look like the competent boyfriend I wanted to be. But most of me didn't care about that. Something in me was sure if I only saw him, I would feel better.

The door opened, my octopus riled, and I hummed, trying to keep myself from falling apart.

The sun was setting outside, and there is a window outside our door, so when Jeremey came in, he was a shadow with white-orange light all around him. With my sensitivity on such high alert it felt like a rush of electricity, as if I'd touched a light socket, but then he shut the door and I could see him normally. Except he was still beautiful to me. Beautiful, soft, tender, perfect Jeremey, my Jeremey, his smile fading as he saw me, his expression becoming complex and then turning into *concerned* as he quickly undid Mai's harness and vest and crossed the room to me.

"Emmet—Emmet, are you all right?"

He stood before me, so close I could almost feel his breath, but he didn't touch me. His eyes were focused with fear, moving all over my body, trying to find out why I was upset. Despite his panic, though, he took such care with me. He knew just how to be with me. He kept his voice quiet. He came close but didn't overstimulate. He was worried but didn't run for help, not until I told him to or he saw that I was in trouble.

Maybe I had more than one sensory sack. Maybe I had a Mai too.

Except I couldn't decide if I wanted to snuggle in the sack or talk to it. I decided to try talking, though with as upset as I was, I was going to have to sign. *I'm sad and overwhelmed. I don't think we can beat RJ King.*

Jeremey could have spoken his reply, but he signed anyway. *We haven't tried yet.*

I can't find the formula. I think the formula only works if you're a liar and a cheat. I don't want to be a liar and a cheat. I don't want to be like him. The tightness in my throat burst out, and a loud, ugly sob rattled the silence of the room. I shut my eyes and kept signing. *But I don't want The Roosevelt Project to fail.*

Another sob followed, and for a moment I gave into crying because it was all I could do. Then I felt hands move over my arms, not touching but disturbing the air above them.

"Emmet, can I hug you?"

I nodded, still crying. I didn't want a hug, but I wanted Jeremey, and this was the way he would be with me now. He hugged me tight, carefully, the same way he handled the rest of me. The hug didn't comfort me much, but thinking about how thoughtfully Jeremey executed the hug made me feel loved, and it helped calm me.

Jeremey kissed me, a soft, firm touch, his lips pressed to my cheek. He pulled away, and he spoke, his voice quiet.

"I don't know how to beat King, or if we can. But I know I want to try. I also know I could never do it on my own. Only with you and the others. But mostly you, Emmet. I can do a lot of things now with Mai. But with you? When you're with me, Emmet Washington, I always feel as if I could do anything in the world. Even if it scares me." He kissed me again, this time closer to my lips. "I don't think you have to lie or cheat, either. I don't think you should. I think if we put our message out there, people will be impressed and believe in us and do the right thing."

This was the part where I always got so tangled inside, where all I could do was think about what new evil algorithm King was using. "What is our message? How will it beat King's math?"

"Our message is everyone deserves a chance to grow and live in the world, to have safe space. We have a program for how people with special needs can have that place, and it's affordable for tax payers."

I considered this a moment. "I think this is an accurate but awkward message."

"It's not an easy thing to paraphrase, no. It's not an easy thing to *do*." Jeremey put his head on my shoulder. "Do you remember when I told you managing my anxiety and depression was like trying to carry an ocean? I feel as if The Roosevelt Project is the same thing, but bigger. We're carrying everyone else's oceans too. It's a lot of oceans."

My octopus was still wobbly, but it liked Jeremey, and it was calm enough I could think about his simile. "We aren't carrying the oceans. We're helping them find places to be to carry them themselves more easily."

"We're trying to shelter the sea, then."

I shut my eyes and imagined this, Jeremey and Darren and David and Kaya and me standing on a beach, holding our oceans while we guarded other people like us as they scooped up their waters and found a place to stand. "It's good. But I don't think people would understand it if we put it on a poster, and I don't know if it would make them call their representatives."

Jeremey picked up my hand, threading our fingers together. "But it will help *you*. You can put it on a poster inside your head, and whenever RJ King makes you angry or you feel defeated, remember you're helping to shelter the sea. It's a big, impossible job, but you already know how to carry an ocean, so it's not such a big deal after all."

My heart felt full, my headache fading, my octopus settling in the haze of happiness. "I love you, Jeremey."

"I love you too, Emmet." He touched the center of my chest, right beside my heart. "Will you make love to me? Right now?"

I wanted to make love to him, but I also wanted to

ask him to marry me. I was so full of love for him in that moment I wanted to ask him right there. I knew he would say yes. I knew too all my fears were silly, and there was no reason not to ask him.

Except I thought about the way Jeremey had taken such care with me. How right now he was aware my autism might mean I would say no and I couldn't have sex with him right now because I was overstimulated.

How Jeremey would like to be proposed to?

It didn't matter to me how it happened because it was just a question, and now that I knew I wanted to do it, his agreement was all I needed, but I wondered what kind of care I should put into asking for Jeremey.

I didn't know the answer to this question yet, except I knew it should be more special than simply asking him in the middle of my breakdown.

Instead I pushed through my stimulation as much as I could as I replied to him, touching his face, kissing him softly on the lips though it made my whole body feel as if there were wooly bears crawling all over me. "Yes, I would like to make love to you right now." I tried to speak in a sexy whisper, but I had a feeling it wasn't as good of a sexy whisper as I wanted it to be.

If Jeremey thought so, he didn't tell me. He shivered and shut his eyes, his body almost going limp. "*Emmet.*"

I wasn't sure how long I could keep doing this, but I decided I would try. "Take care of Mai while I clean up in the bathroom, then meet me in my room. Then

I'll make love to you some more." I kissed him softly again, telling the octopus to make friends with the wooly bears.

CHAPTER FOURTEEN

Jeremey

THERE WAS SOMETHING different about Emmet as he made love to me.

It wasn't bad, and it wasn't so odd I felt as if someone else was having sex with me, but I noticed we weren't having the sex we usually had. It wasn't as if we always did the exact same thing, but Emmet does have his patterns and habits, and, well, we have them in bed too. This was more than that, though. It was the *way* he was having sex with me that felt different. I liked it, but it was so unexpected I couldn't stop thinking about it.

He was so *gentle*. Emmet has a thing about pressure and the way he touches me. When it's too soft it overstimulates him. I worried he wouldn't be able to have sex at all because he'd been so upset in the living room, and any contact might have been too much.

So why was he running his hands over my skin, so soft and faint I tingled all over? His lips on my collarbone were bare brushes, teases and whispers—this should be making *his* skin crawl, but he didn't stop, didn't say anything. It was something out of my deepest fantasy, but I couldn't enjoy it. All I could think about was how out of character it was for him, how it went against everything I knew him to be, and eventually I couldn't take it anymore. I put my hands on his shoulders and looked him in the eye.

"Emmet, what's going on? Why are you being so soft?"

He frowned. "Am I doing it wrong?"

I couldn't stop a shiver. "No. It's wonderful—but *you* can't be enjoying it, can you? You always tell me this is the kind of touch you can't stand. That it almost hurts you."

"But you like it. I wanted you to have it this time."

My heart ached and melted at the same time. "I don't want you to hurt for me. It isn't pleasure for me if it hurts you."

He ran his hand down my sternum, the contact soft but more firm, an Emmet touch again. "It doesn't hurt exactly. More of a tickle."

I touched him too, being pointed in giving him the sensation I knew *he* enjoyed. "Have I ever complained about your touches? Have I said I wished for something different?"

He was staring at my hairline, but I knew he was looking as directly into my eyes as he could. "You like them. You should get them sometimes. And I don't want anyone else to give them to you."

My heart swelled, and I pulled him closer to me, so his chest was pressed to mine as I spoke into his ear. "But don't you see, Emmet? All I want is you. It's as if you're the cake and everything else is frosting. I don't want any other cake but you."

He pushed up on his elbows and smiled his sideways Emmet smile. "I'm a cake?"

I had expected him to tell me he didn't like similes. "Yes. You're my cake."

"I don't want to get eaten."

I blushed, but I made myself say the words. "No. I want *you* to eat *me* up." I pressed on, past the embarrassment. It was Emmet. I had nothing to fear. "I don't want you to try to change for me. I only want to be with you as you are. I'll do whatever you want me to do. I enjoy it when you touch me soft or hard, when you kiss me or hold me or simply lie beside me. When you're in the mood to kiss me all over and drive me wild or when you need to be alone and I only can sit outside your door, loving you. That's what I want from you, Emmet. For you to let me be with you and help you. I don't ever want you to change for me."

For a moment his gaze met mine, and I stilled, thrilling. He was so intense I felt pinned to the bed. "You're my sensory sack."

"Your what?"

"My sensory sack. Like at the City Council meeting, when The Roosevelt Blues Brothers closed in for me, but this time it's just you. You're better than them.

You're the best sensory sack of all. Better sometimes than the real thing."

I didn't know what he meant at first, and then I realized. His sack in the closet. I was his...sack, his place to go for comfort. "Yes. Let me be your sensory sack. Let me be your safe place, where you can be yourself, where you can calm yourself, or whatever you need me to be. Come inside me, Emmet, and let me make the world go away."

It was as if my words unbuckled something in him. He came at me with all his carefulness stripped away, no longer trying to be smooth and tender. I had enjoyed the other, but I preferred this. I wasn't worried about him faking anything for me, not when he behaved this way.

His kiss was clumsy, overeager, and so full of Emmet I melted. I opened my mouth and took him in, feeling myself dissolve away as I let him move me into the position he wanted on the bed. I enjoyed, though, the way he trembled as he shifted my body, the way he was in control but only barely. Or rather, he was in control, but he wasn't disciplining his body the way he did in public. He hummed and rocked and jerked, all his autistic tics on full display, and each one warmed my heart, undoing me further as he undressed me, caressed me, got me ready for him.

Yes, my love. Let me see you, all of you.

This was the same Emmet I had discovered when I came into the apartment with Mai, complete with all the aspects of his autism that so often frustrated him, except right now Emmet moved *with* his disabilities, made them work for him instead of fighting them. Danced with his octopus instead of letting it strangle him. And I knew I was biased. My love colored my vision, but to me this Emmet was so beautiful, so handsome, so perfect. I would never want him to be anyone other than who he was. If someone invented a technology that could make his brain like brains on the mean, could make him behave the same as other men without all the tics and habits setting him apart, I would still love him, but it would break my heart too, because I would miss this Emmet.

I can't beat you either, RJ King, I thought, shutting my eyes as Emmet placed his mouth on my neck, *but I can do this. I can lift up this man, the one who's already bested you once. I can shine for him, keep him safe, keep him happy. I don't have many strengths, but I do have this. Watch me, King. Watch me shore him up. Watch me make him as strong as I can, so he can take you down.*

As Emmet made love to me, I imagined I was a liquid sheath, that as he stroked and entered my body I enveloped him right back, putting a protective coating around him and sending all my energy into him, feeding his octopus and strengthening his walls, fueling the computers in his brilliant mind. I let my love pour into him, trying to empty myself, except the more I pushed into him, the more power and strength and love I found inside myself. The idea that my love and our power together was endless thrilled me, and I gasped, clutching at him, imagining so long as we were together, nothing bad would ever happen.

I knew, intellectually, this wasn't true. But in that moment it *felt* true. And as we lay in his bed together after, Emmet holding me though I knew he was overstimulated, I swam in the rush of endorphins, knowing for at least a little while they would douse my anxiety and depression better than any drug could ever hope to attempt.

I opened my eyes lazily, my lids heavy as I resisted the urge to stroke Emmet's abdomen, staring across his naked chest instead. "If you need to go rock in the living room, I understand. It's okay."

"I don't need to. You're my sensory sack. The octopus is fine, with you."

I shut my eyes again, heady with the rush of emotion. "Okay," I replied, because it was all I could manage.

Then I held still, as still as I could, lying beside him as my love spun a more protective web around him. Because I was going to be the best sensory sack Emmet had ever had.

CHAPTER FIFTEEN

Emmet

OUR FIRST EVENT was planned for the last Saturday in April at the Dallas County Fairgrounds.

Kaya and the team from marketing helping our project did a lot of the technical setting up of the venue, making sure we had the right lighting and sound. They also promoted our appearance and made sure people were coming, though Darren helped with all of this stuff too. Every other aspect, though, The Roosevelt Blues Brothers team handled alone. We selected Dallas County as our target area for our first run outside of Ames, and we elected to use the fairgrounds as our test-run venue.

"It makes the most sense on both counts," David said. "West Des Moines is a little conservative, but not completely, and they have money. They're our target demographic. Plus my dad has a ton of connections there. He can work the crowd while we put on our show."

Darren made a sign indicating he wanted to speak, and we waited while he typed into his pad. "We want to give them the speech too, right?"

"Oh yeah. And the brochures, the slide show, the whole works. But I think they want the song and dance too." David shifted his upper body in his chair, grinning his sly grin. "Especially for the West Des Moines crowd. You're talking *prime* money there. We might not only get votes. We might get donors for the foundation. Because we might as well kill two birds with one stone."

Jeremey frowned. "Foundation?"

David's smile got bigger, and it changed. His nose crinkled, and his eyes narrowed. "I forgot my dad didn't tell you guys yet. He filed the paperwork with the lawyer yesterday. There's going to be a Roosevelt Foundation now too, in addition to the project. The foundation is where all the money will go when it gets donated, and hopefully eventually it will become an education and information arm of The Roosevelt Project. He and Kaya want it to become independent and self-perpetuating, but it's going to take a bit of work. And capital. It'll be nonprofit, but it'll need some money to make the wheels go around. Which is why this Dallas County performance is such a good start. We'll never make enough money in donations to reach our goal. Maybe to keep The Roosevelt solvent, but never to help establish a network of Roosevelts across the state. But that doesn't mean I'm not going to bat my eyelashes at rich people and try to get them to empty their wallets at me. This chair isn't good for a whole lot, but if I can use it to raise money for our cause, I'm going balls to the wall."

I wasn't sure what balls David was putting to the wall and why, and I thought about asking him, but Kaya came over to us and told us the tech crew was ready for us to rehearse, so I didn't say anything. We needed a lot of practice still, after all.

We weren't bad, but we'd decided we wanted to be more polished than we'd been for the Target flash mob, which meant more rehearsal. We had better costumes this time, which was nice. All four of us had suits, but they were fitted by a real tailor and they all matched. The hats were my favorite part. They were soft and had a secret strip of grip padding in the front so when we removed them for our dance moves they didn't fall out of our hands as easily. David didn't take his off himself, because it was too difficult for him to execute the gesture in time to the beat, so I took it off for him, and it was easier for me to grab it with the grip strip. Kaya had come up with the idea, and she asked a haberdasher to put the strip in as a special feature. I didn't know we had a haberdasher in Iowa until she drove us to Des Moines to meet him. He was a nice older man who was excited we all wanted custom hats.

Our musical number was a great deal of work, but I didn't mind because I got to be Elwood Blues again. Lip-syncing is hard, but "Try Everything" is a good song. I'm not a female singer, so people are suspending their disbelief more than usual, but Kaya says we're so good it doesn't matter.

I have fun with this because I don't only pretend to sing, I dance with Jeremey. The last time we did a lip sync he had a difficult time simply participating, but he's come a long way with his social anxiety now, and he says being on stage with lights blasting into his face helps a lot because they block out the audience and he can't see them at all. His biggest struggle is getting out of bed if he's having a bad bout of depression, but Mai helps him there. Also he says having Mai on stage (she's also has a costume, a special jacket and hat) makes it okay, though he's best when he's with me. In fact if he holds my hand, he can lip sync and dance. So for most of the time he's either holding Mai's leash or dancing with me.

There's one part of the number where we sing into the microphone together, another where we each have our own mics, and one part where I spin him around. Usually I prefer to dance by myself, and I do have a great dance solo where I do my Elwood Blues dance because Kaya says it's my signature move and I need to include it, but I like the part where I dance with Jeremey better. I enjoy the way he blushes and looks at me like it doesn't matter how big an audience we have, when I'm spinning him, there's nobody else in the world but the two of us.

Darren does some dancing too, but he prefers to

stay in place when he dances. He has enough mobility and balance issues that he doesn't want to move too much on stage, and David of course needs to stay in his chair. So Darren and David do their own version of a dance together, where David spins his chair and Darren spins in place. Mostly though they run their own kind of show, as David calls it. David flirts with the audience and with Darren, and Darren signs the lyrics of the song as he does his dance. He uses ASL as much as he can, not his special sign, but he had to choose which parts of the lyrics he would sign, because he can't do all the signs right, since his hands won't always behave, sometimes not going fast enough and sometimes they simply won't do the sign properly at all.

We've had audiences a lot of the time at our rehearsals, though the fairgrounds would be our first official performance. At first we performed for the staff at Workiva, but eventually Kaya arranged for us to give private practice concerts at City Hall for the council, Bob Loris's crew, some of the donors we already had on board, and some other people Dr. North found who he thought would be good for us to practice on. This included our parents.

My mom had come to one of the Workiva practices, but when she came backstage after the City Hall dress rehearsal, she hugged me too tight and cried. "My baby boy is all grown up," she kept saying, which didn't make any sense because I have been grown up for some time, and there was nothing about dancing and pretending to sing on a stage in downtown Ames that made me any more grown up. But mostly I needed her to stop hugging me so tight.

"Mom, stop."

She did, but she kissed me on the cheek first. My dad didn't hug me, but he smiled a bigger smile than usual and told me he was proud of me with his extra-soft voice. My aunt Althea came too, and she didn't hug me, but she said she thought our costumes were good and she could tell I'd practiced.

"We have. This was a lot of work. But it's been fun."

Jeremey stood beside me too. He touched two fingers to my wrist and tapped twice, his silent question to hold my hand. I touched his fingers, telling him yes, I would hold hands with him now. He laced our fingers together and held my hand tight in his as he spoke to my family. "I hope everyone at the show at the fairgrounds likes it too. I hope it makes them join our cause."

"It will." This was Kaya, and she had a proud face on as she came to join us. "Dallas County will be the first performance in a long line of performances, but it's going to be worth it, and in the end we're going to win. RJ King is going to rue the day he tangled with The Roosevelt Blues Brothers."

I still wasn't sure about this, but I hoped she was right.

We kept practicing at The Roosevelt, but soon it

was time for us to get in the van with Kaya and go to Adel and get ready for our event. I didn't get nervous until we were on the road, or at least I hadn't realized how nervous I was until we were on the road. I hummed and rocked to calm myself, but I had a great deal of nervousness, and my octopus was especially slippery.

Jeremey sat beside me. He didn't take my hand, was careful not to touch me, but he spoke quietly to me, being my sensory sack. He didn't tell me how we'd be fine. He talked about other things, taking my mind off it. He pointed out things he saw on the road, other cars, talked about restaurants we might try in Des Moines. "We could go to Zombie Burger. I always wanted to go there."

Darren held up his iPad, and we waited while he typed. "It's quite busy there, according to the Internet. Tough to get a table. No reservations either."

"But they have the one out at the mall now," David pointed out. "We could get it there and eat in the food court. And if people didn't want to eat at Zombie Burger, they would have other options."

Would the mall be too busy for you? I signed to Jeremey.

He signed back, *Not with Mai.*

Mai was curled on the seat beside him, asleep. He had her vest off because she didn't have to work at the moment, and she was more comfortable with it off. She got tired after performances, and he wanted to let her rest now as much as she could.

The event was going to be hard on Mai no matter what we did, however. I knew there was no way around that. "We should get her a treat after we finish."

Jeremey smiled. "She'd like that."

Darren signed to speak and then held up his iPad again after he typed. "There's a store in the mall with treats for dogs."

"Sounds great." Jeremey stroked Mai's head, rubbing behind her ears. "You're an expert on Jordan Creek Mall, Darren. Have you been there a lot?"

We waited while Darren typed his answer. "I've never been there, but I've done a great deal of research online." He paused to type some more. "I want to explore it when we're done eating if we have some spare time."

"I'm down for some mall cruising." David craned his neck as much as he could toward us. "Will you let me be your wingman, D-man?"

Darren held out his fist and bumped David awkwardly in the shoulder in reply, adding a happy grunt for emphasis.

Kaya reached for the radio and pushed a CD into the player. "Okay, Emmet, you said you wanted to start warming up when we were fifteen minutes away, and I think that's about how close we are. You guys ready to get your jam on?"

We said we were, and I appreciated the way our voices sounded—Jeremey's blended with mine, his *Ready* tangling with my *Yes* over the top of Darren's excited bark and David's deep *Let's do this thing.* It was as if we were already singing. Mai made a small whine too, waking up and wondering why everyone was so excited, though she calmed when Jeremey stroked her fur.

In the performances we never sing, but in the van we do. We weren't on-key, because only Jeremey and Kaya can hit the notes properly, and Darren can't get the words out, but we enjoy making the sound. Darren's favorite parts are the *oh, oh, oh, oh, oh-s* because he's good at them, though sometimes he gets excited and does too many or starts laughing or hissing or rocking too hard. It's okay though, because it's a Roosevelt Blues Brothers jam. There aren't any rules.

Kaya kept the song on repeat all the way to the fairgrounds, and we stayed in the van to finish it once we'd parked.

Then it was time to go inside, get into our costumes, and get ready.

The plan was for us to wait backstage while Kaya and a few other people from Workiva helped Bob prep the room. We'd had a big meeting about it, and we'd decided this first time it would be best for the four of us to make a big entrance before we gave our presentation. Kaya had invited the local news stations and newspapers, and she came backstage before she went out to let us know the room was full of cameras and reporters, and we should expect lots of lights and flashes when we went out.

"It's a full house. Bob came through with his contacts." She seemed happy, but worried, especially as she looked at Jeremey. "Will you guys be okay with so many people?"

Jeremey nodded. "I've been practicing my breathing, and Mai has been comforting me. She knows I'm uneasy, and we're working together. I can't promise I'll be fine, but I'm doing my best, and I believe I can do it."

Kaya hugged him, then David, then made the hug sign to Darren and me. "I'm so proud of you guys. You're going to be fantastic, I just know it. And you *look* amazing. Dan Aykroyd would think he was staring at a mirror, Emmet."

I did a little of my Elwood Blues dance, then smiled.

It was difficult to wait, because we got nervous with nothing to do but listen to the murmur of the crowd and Kaya's and Bob's voices. I could hear what they were saying, mostly, but even with my super hearing it was difficult to make out individual words. Jeremey hugged Mai, burying his face in her fur. Darren rocked in his seat, absorbed in a video on his iPad. David didn't do much, only stared at the curtain separating us from the stage where we'd be going out as soon as they told us it was time.

I worried if this was a good idea. I worried if we were good enough to do this. I worried people think we were awkward or weird, not the cool Roosevelt

Blues Brothers we knew we were. I worried they would laugh at us and the magic we always felt when we put on these clothes and sang this song would be taken away.

And then the stage manager told us it was time to go out and go to our places, and I had to tell the octopus to be good, because it was showtime. It hovered over my head, trembling as the curtain parted and the lights hit us.

The music began, and The Roosevelt Blues Brothers did too.

This is why we did all the rehearsals, because there was something about wearing those costumes, our music playing, that made everything okay. We simply followed the song and let it carry us through the routine. At first I simply moved like a robot, but as I saw the audience was excited and happy for us, I relaxed and let my Elwood show, especially when I had my solo dance. I got brave when I danced with Jeremey too, my heart racing as I spun him and dipped him. Darren and David were getting into it as well—we were all having so much fun. So was the audience. It was everything we'd ever wanted the performance to be. People were clapping along and swaying in their seats, smiling at us.

When the song finished, they cheered and stood up, whistling and clapping for a long time. It was time for me to go make my speech, a modified version of what I'd said to the city council, but I couldn't move at first because I was so surprised by how many people were there and how happy they were to see us. How much they enjoyed our dance.

Maybe we have the algorithm after all.

I wasn't sure. But for once my octopus wriggled in excitement, not fear, as I went to stand behind the podium, and when I rocked in place and let out a hum before I approached the mic, it was because I was happy, not because I was scared.

OUR ROOSEVELT BLUES Brothers Tour went well wherever we went.

The format changed after the first performance, and now I came out first and gave my speech before joining the other Brothers on the stage and doing our dance. We often did press interviews afterward, and sometimes we talked to people from the audience, but Bob and Kaya always carefully controlled who approached us and how. David did most of the interviews since he was the most social, though he started keeping Darren with him, insisting he needed his wingman. I began to think he was trying to get people to see Darren as more of a person, because since he was quiet they often ignored him and didn't ask him for interviews. David also made them be patient and wait for Darren to type his replies on his iPad, though sometimes he translated for Darren and read his sign language for the interviewers.

I did some of the interviews too, but usually I was too overstimulated after the speech and the performance to do much and had to schedule them for another time after I recovered. Jeremey didn't do any, not during the events, though he did agree a few times to talk to people about Mai and how she'd helped him with his social anxiety. Dr. North got involved too, not as our therapist but as an expert in the field, talking about the importance of mental health care.

This was my mother's doing. She had been helping too, though not like Bob or Kaya. She'd been building up support for The Roosevelt Foundation by talking to other doctors and people in the medical profession about the importance of a strong mental health network in the state and why we need to stand up for it before it's completely dismantled. So when our first performance got the media interested in writing stories about the importance of mental health facilities and how positive impacts can make a difference in the lives of patients and the communities, my mom was there with experts lined up to do interviews, and one of the most popular people to do those interviews was Dr. North.

I enjoyed listening to his interviews. He sounded the way he did in our sessions, and I wondered if he was giving therapy to the reporters and they didn't know it. I decided this was something he would do but didn't bring it up as I didn't want to point it out and ruin the surprise. There were a number of stories in the news now about our performances and about the mental health facilities closing, a lot of interviews about us. We were a viral Internet hit again, though this time there were all kinds of videos of us, from the Dallas County event, and one in Johnson County, and another in Cedar Falls, and another in Fairfield.

We did a great deal of traveling in April and May, and I did get somewhat tired of it, but it was an important cause, and so I did my best to accept it. Sometimes we had to stay in a hotel, which wasn't as nice, but I always roomed with Jeremey which was fun. He preferred the hotels, especially when they were bed and breakfasts and we had fancy rooms, but most of the time we had to stay at actual hotels because the bed and breakfasts weren't accessible enough for David's chair.

When we were in eastern Iowa, Darren got excited because he knew a lot more about everything since this was where he grew up. I did too, but I hadn't been there as long as he was, and his parents still lived there. We also stopped and saw Darren's family, who were happy to see us. They hugged David and Bob too, and they cried as they thanked Bob for giving Darren a better place to stay. Bob didn't cry, but his voice was gruff and his eyes damp as he told them he was doing all he could to get more young adults such as Darren a safe place to live.

We stayed at Darren's house in Iowa City, some of us anyway. David went to a hotel with his dad and

Kaya, but Jeremey and Darren and I stayed at Darren's house. Darren showed us his old room and his computer collection, toys, and the things he'd collected. He'd always enjoyed tech, especially computers, and he had some interesting pieces, including some old hardware from the 1980s that couldn't access the Internet. He showed us some fun 8-bit games and computer software programs that used to be advanced but were less complicated than a coffee maker nowadays.

Mai liked Darren's house because they had a fenced-in backyard, and she and Jeremey had fun while Darren's family barbecued. While the family cooked and Jeremey and Mai played, Darren signed me a story about something he'd read online, about a girl with cerebral palsy who lived in Connecticut who had been almost killed by her grandparents when her parents had left her with them for too long.

Why did they try to kill her? I signed this to him, because he was using his iPad to show me the news article. *Did she do something bad?*

No. But her disability is severe, and they were tired of caring for her, and the parents kept leaving her behind with the grandparents while the parents went away on vacations. The grandparents got overwhelmed and angry, and when they couldn't get anyone else to help take care of the granddaughter, they decided they would get rid of her themselves. They tried to make it look as if it were an accident. They wanted the insurance money and to not have to deal with the hassle anymore.

I thought of how much of a hassle I had been when I was young, how I had kicked and hit and bit and slammed my head into walls until I'd been able to control my octopus better. I felt sad and had to hum and rock. *Those are bad people, those grandparents. I hope they go to jail.*

I think they will, but, Emmet, this is another problem The Roosevelt Blues Brothers need to help. There are too many people who think it's okay to hurt people like us, to call us burdens, to tease us and kick us and try to kill us. Even people who are supposed to love us. Once we win with RJ King and the legislature, can we try to do something about this?

Sometimes I still wasn't sure we were going to win, but I didn't want to be negative and say so. I nodded and signed yes too for emphasis. *You know we'll keep fighting. We're The Roosevelt Blues Brothers. Nothing can stop us.* I didn't know how we could help people like this girl yet, but we could find a way. When I was with the Blues Brothers and Kaya and Bob, I felt as if I could do anything.

Darren barked a laugh and held his hand up for a high-five. I met it and grinned back, and then we sat together, rocking as we watched our friends and families have a quiet evening.

I didn't always enjoy the traveling. I missed my apartment and my train tracks and my routine, but I enjoyed believing we were doing something important, that though I couldn't put it into a formula, it seemed as if an algorithm was working. We did have some data, the number of people who had joined the foundation as donors and people who had pledged to call their representatives, and Kaya had been in contact with another, more political organization tracking the projected vote totals for the bill. It was complicated because they had to lobby the representatives and the senators both, though the strategy they were using was to kill the measure in the lower chamber so it didn't go higher. What Kaya said was if it passed the Iowa House, it would definitely pass the senate and be signed by the governor. So we had to stop it now, or there would be no stopping it.

Everyone kept telling me they were sure we would win, that the bill wouldn't pass, and I wanted to believe them. But to be honest the fact that we had to lip sync and dance and I had to keep giving speeches and put Darren's and my autism and David's quadriplegia and Jeremey's social anxiety on display to get people's attention made me realize how much people had been ignoring us all this time. I had been aware of this truth my whole life, but our tour helped me see it in a new way, and sometimes I felt hopeless and angry. Why did I have to get on a stage and perform to get the same rights as other people? Part of me thought it didn't matter, this was what I had to do to win, and then I wondered if I was another version of RJ King, if this was me cheating on the algorithm.

I asked Dr. North about it in therapy, and I could tell my question surprised him. His eyebrows quivered, and he put his hand over his mouth, which is his big-thinking gesture. I rocked and waited for him to answer.

"An astute observation," he said at last. "But no, I don't think it makes you the same as RJ King, not in the way you imply. There is some similarity, I suppose, in that you both manipulate public opinion for your own use. But this is true in essentially all communication. I'm manipulating your thoughts right now. The key, however, is I go to great lengths to invite you to consider possibilities, not scold or lure you into false ideals. For example, I would ask you to think about the difference between your presentation and King's. *Your* part of the presentation in particular. You offer your story and your feelings, and then you step aside, inviting people to make their own choices. You do your best to present a compelling argument, yes. But then you don't remain involved. How do you think King compares to how I see your method?"

I considered this. "King is more aggressive. He tells people how to think. It doesn't sound as if this is what he's doing, but I've watched him a lot. Darren discovered videos of him at events online. He uses his smile like a weapon. People who are moved by social cues are distracted by it and don't notice that when he smiles he's telling them how to think and feel."

"I would agree with you, having met the man myself. Is his behavior similar to how you think you behave at your events for the foundation?"

"*Hmmm.* No." I rocked and hummed some more, the simple idea of such a thing upsetting to me.

"Then no, Emmet. I don't think you're anything like RJ King."

I decided Dr. North was right, and it made me feel better. I had another question for him, though, and I hoped he would be able to be as much help with this one as well. "I also wanted to talk to you about proposing to Jeremey."

Dr. North smiled bigger. "Yes? Have you decided you're ready?"

"Yes. But I also decided I need to make it special for Jeremey when I ask, except I don't know how to do it."

He leaned back in his chair. "Special how? What do you mean?"

"Jeremey is sentimental. I'm not, and I don't need anything fancy to happen when I ask him to marry me, but I think Jeremey would enjoy it. Except every time I try to come up with something he'd like, I end up rocking and humming in my sensory sack."

"Have you tried talking to your mother about this? Or are you trying to *not* talk to your mother about this?"

"You know my mother. She would get too excited. Plus it doesn't feel grown up to have her helping."

"I'll allow you this point. Though I would advise you to let her help with the wedding. She excels at that kind of planning, and neither you nor Jeremey will find the finer details of it to your liking." He tapped his finger on the side of his cheek. "Well, let's break it down. What are the types of things you know you need to include, and avoid, in your proposal for Jeremey?"

"It needs to be romantic, but not busy or crowded. In fact I think it would be better if it were only the two of us."

"There, that's one part of the decision made or narrowed. Somewhere private. All right, we have private and romantic. Next element?"

What else would Jeremey want? "He would want Mai to be there."

"Arranging Mai's presence would be easy enough. What else?"

It was tough work, and he asked me a lot of questions, but the questions made me think, and in the end I had a good idea of what I wanted to do, how I would ask Jeremey. Now all I had to do was make the arrangements and actually do the asking.

"Thank you, Dr. North. This conversation was helpful."

"My pleasure. Do you have rings chosen, or will you save those for the ceremony?"

"I have rings, engagements bands, and wedding bands to add for the wedding picked out. I haven't bought them, but I know what I want to purchase." Jeremey would want something on his hand while we waited to get married, and I did too. If he didn't want them, we could exchange them, but I knew Jeremey would appreciate the ones I'd picked out. I knew what he liked.

"Then the best of luck to you. Except I'm quite certain you'll have no trouble getting the answer you want out of your young man." He winked at me.

I didn't wink back, but I smiled as big as I could. Because I was pretty certain too.

CHAPTER SIXTEEN

Jeremey

EMMET WAS UP to something.

I didn't know what, but he was planning something, no question, and I was fairly sure it didn't have anything to do with The Roosevelt Project for a change. We were still doing events on the weekends, but not as many as we had been—it was June now and the legislative session had been extended because they hadn't voted on several key pieces of legislation, including the bill deciding mental health funding. We'd decided to keep up our lobbying efforts but tone them down ever so slightly so as to save our energy before the big vote, when we'd make another push. "Stay relevant but don't drown the issue," was what Kaya kept saying.

So what Emmet was so busy rushing around for, being secretive and flustered about, I had no idea, but he roped other people into it too plenty of times, and I'll be honest, I was jealous. He whispered with Darren or David and even Sally and Tammy, and I didn't know why or what for. When I asked him what was going on, he gave me the hand sign meaning he didn't want to talk about it, but that upset me since he was talking to every other person in our lives about it, just not me.

Everyone else ran off on secret missions with Emmet, and I ended up sitting in the lounge or out on the playground equipment, where I ran into Stuart a number of times. I didn't mind Stuart, not the way I know Emmet did. Stuart was younger than we were, but not by much. He had autism too, and he was even more nonverbal than Darren, more severely locked inside himself and unable to communicate. When we'd first moved into The Roosevelt, he'd mostly screamed in order to speak, but now he got right up into people's faces, breathing heavy and staring into space beside their heads.

Stuart was intense, yes, and Mai often had to remind him to give me personal space, but it didn't bother me to be with him. I have a soft spot for autistic people now, having made friends with so many, having fallen in love with someone with autism, though Emmet's autism is so different. The thing is, Emmet is different, and he isn't. Sometimes when I sit with Stuart, I feel as if I can see Emmet in him. I can't help wondering if Emmet and Stuart aren't more alike than they are different. I don't know why I think that, but I do.

I half-waited for Emmet to comment on how

much time I was spending with Stuart, but whatever he was working on had him too distracted to notice. I almost asked Emmet directly what he was up to. But then one day when I woke up from my nap, I saw a message from Emmet beside my bed, printed in the special font he uses for the notes he leaves for me.

Meet me on the roof, and bring Mai.

I frowned at the piece of paper. The roof? Of the building? Of The Roosevelt? I didn't know we *could* go up there. How did I do that? But when I got out of bed, before I could think of who I would ask to figure this out, or before I could find my phone to text him, I saw another note, this one on top of a towel on my dresser.

Take a shower.

I smiled and picked up the towel, and then…well, I took a shower. This was an old game, Emmet telling me what to do, and I played it, because I knew if I kept following his commands, there would be new instructions, and eventually one of them would lead me to the roof. Indeed, when I got out of the shower, on the back of the door was a suit—not my Blues Brothers suit but another nice one, this one a soft gray with a pink tie. It wasn't something I would have picked out for myself, but I appreciated it.

Wear this, the note said. So I did.

I followed notes all through the house, guiding me into shoes and cufflinks and putting a leash on Mai to bring her along as we went down the hall and to a door

I had thought led to storage but it turned out opened to a set of stairs taking me to the roof. The stairs were creaky and dimly lit, making me uneasy, but as I neared the top I heard music playing, and when I opened the door, I saw little white lights, the type you put on Christmas trees, except these were all white even on the strands, and they were wrapped in tulle. They covered the archway by the door, some posts in the center, and as I came around the corner, I saw another arch, this one something someone had clearly put up, something that couldn't possibly be on the roof on a regular basis. It had more white lights and tulle and a sort of sheet over the top, and fake ivy, and behind it the sun was setting, making the world appear as if it were set in a movie or a fairy tale.

Underneath the arch, wearing a suit matching mine, calm and handsome and more beautiful than anything I had ever seen in the whole world, was my Emmet.

He smiled as he saw me, a very Emmet smile, slightly crooked and too wide, his gaze fixed just above my head. "Hello, Jeremey."

My heart soared. "Hello, Emmet. This is beautiful. But why are we on the roof, and why is it decorated like this? Are we having some kind of party?"

"I'll explain it to you, but you need to come closer. I have something I need to tell you, and something I need to ask you."

He led me to the edge of the building to gaze out over the neighborhood. My heart fluttered as my mind raced, trying to figure out what might be going on.

"Do you see the street down there, the intersection and stretch of road by the yellow house and the clump of trees by the green truck? That's where we met at the block party." Emmet pointed to the space, then to another section of the neighborhood. "And there's your parents' house, and my family's house. Oh, and look, there's the moon, over that tree."

I blinked, certain he had to be wrong, but no, there it was, a pale half shape, hovering over a treetop, blue white and against the sky. "Wow. I didn't notice it was there."

"The moon wanted to come say hello, because this is a big day. All of our important places and things are close by to us up here. Bob has talked about making a rooftop greenhouse for The Roosevelt, and if he does, we could always come up here and see our important places. Except I want to make this roof another important place for us right now. I want it to be the place where I told you how much I love you and how much I always want you in my life, for all of my life."

My insides went gooey, and I squeezed Emmet's hand. "I always want you in my life too. I don't ever want to be without you. I love you so much, Emmet Washington."

Emmet kissed my cheek, a soft brush that made me want to swoon. Then he let go of my hand, went back to where he'd been standing when I came onto the roof, and pulled a small white bag from his pocket.

"Mai."

Mai's ears perked up. She was trained to listen to Emmet's commands too.

"Mai, take it."

Mai checked with me, and once I set her free from her leash, she went, collecting the bag from Emmet.

"Go give it to Jeremey."

She brought the bag carefully to me in her mouth, releasing it to me when I asked her to drop it. I opened it with shaking hands as Emmet closed the distance between us once more. The bag was tied with gold string, and when I undid the knot, I tipped the bag upside down and emptied the contents into my palm.

A pair of rings fell out.

Emmet took one of them and held it over the tip of the fourth finger of my left hand, though he didn't slip it on. "Jeremey Andrew Samson, will you marry me?"

The world, already subdued, grew gentler still, so tender and fragile and perfect I wasn't sure I could breathe. I stared at the ring hovering over my finger, felt the weight of its companion in my palm. Realized what Emmet had asked me, what was happening to me, that it was real, and my emotions were such an overwhelming sea I thought I might drown in them.

As always, Emmet was my anchor. He reached for me before Mai could sense the riot inside me, touching my arm with his free hand. "Did I do it wrong? I'm sorry. I tried to make it a proposal you would like."

The idea that he thought I didn't like this stirred me out of my frozen state. I shook my head, drawing a low, deep breath to calm myself before I attempted to speak. "I love it. It's perfect. So perfect it overwhelmed me for a moment." I squeezed my hand around the ring in my palm—Emmet's ring, the one he had given to me—and drew another breath as I lifted my gaze to his, or rather I looked into his eyes, which were still focused above me. "Yes, Emmet. I would love very much to marry you. Thank you for asking me in such a wonderful way."

He slipped the ring onto my finger, past the knuckle until it was snug in its place at the end, glinting in the twilight. "I measured your handprint to make sure the size would fit."

I recalled the activity Sally had suggested a few weeks ago one Saturday, a handprint collage on the lounge wall, how they'd gently bullied me into making a handprint too, and I smiled to myself. "You had a lot of help, getting this set up."

"Yes. I told you. I wanted to give you a proposal you enjoyed."

Because Emmet wouldn't have needed any of this. He would have been content to ask me at the dinner table, so long as we weren't actively consuming food at the time. He truly had done this for my sake, down to asking Mai to bring me the ring. I was moved all over again, and had to pause to wipe tears from my eyes. "Here. Let me put your ring on you too."

The rings weren't gold. They were a kind of silvery color, and they had a wavy blue line across the middle filled with sapphires, like an ocean.

"There are bands that fit on them," Emmet explained as I slid the ring on his finger. "For when we get married. But I wanted us to wear rings now, so we could think about being engaged each time we looked at our hands. I thought you would appreciate that part. And I would enjoy it too."

He was correct. I did like it. I loved all of it, everything he was giving me. *I love you, Emmet.* "The rings are beautiful. Did you pick them out yourself?"

"Yes. At Ames Silversmithing. They said if you didn't care for them, we can get different ones. But I thought I could guess which ones you would prefer and you would enjoy the surprise better than making the decision."

"You thought right." My heart swelled, so full I thought it would burst. "I love you so much."

"I love you too."

"May I kiss you, Emmet?"

He kissed me instead, leaning in to press his lips to mine, sweetly at first, then teasing his tongue against mine to kiss me more deeply. We had gotten quite good at kissing since we first started, knew how to do the dance with each other, and yet no kiss had ever been quite like this one: a kiss on a rooftop to seal our engagement.

Married. I was going to get married.

To Emmet.

The distant blare of a train horn cut through the moment, then sounded once more as the train came closer, and I lifted my head toward the source of the disturbance. Emmet turned as well, a look of pleasure on his face, and I laughed.

"You knew this train was coming, didn't you? You timed the proposal to happen when it would come by."

His smile widened, and he kept his gaze on the tracks, where the engine had appeared around the gap in the trees. "Not *all* of the proposal was for you."

I put my arm around his waist, leaned on his shoulder, easing against him with careful pressure, letting my heart float into the clouds as my dog arranged herself on top of my feet and the train rolled slowly past. "I'm glad," I replied, and settled in to watch.

CHAPTER SEVENTEEN

Emmet

I ENJOYED BEING engaged, mostly.

The trouble was dealing with people finding out I was engaged. Jeremey's parents were uncomfortable. He hadn't had much contact with them since he moved out of their house because of their rocky past relationship, and Dr. North had said he thought it was a good idea. I did too. But when we got engaged, Jeremey insisted he had to meet with them. "How could I get married and not tell them?"

So we went to tell them, and it was awkward. They've never liked me, and they didn't like me that day either. They don't think I'm a whole person because I have autism, and they think Jeremey should be with someone better. Dr. North said also they didn't want to see Jeremey growing up, but I think mostly they don't want him growing up with someone with autism. I wish we could have skipped talking to them, but this is part of being an adult. They're going to be my in-laws, and a lot of people have difficult in-laws.

It wasn't only Jeremey's parents who judged us though, and some of them judged Jeremey as much as they did me. This was the problem of our being so public, with all the performances. People saw us everywhere and knew our business, and they left comments on our videos and our social media pages. The word got out about our engagement, and some people thought we shouldn't be getting married, which always made me upset. They were total strangers, faceless and usually nameless, interjecting their thoughts and opinions on our lives and our worth as people. I wasn't supposed to read those comments, but I often did anyway. Jeremey did too, and they upset him more than me. He had to go hug Mai for a long time afterward. There were mentions of the R word and people saying people like us shouldn't get married.

What did they mean, people like us? Who decided they got to judge us?

Mostly, however, people were happy for Jeremey and me, and now when we did our events for the foundation and the project, I could talk about my fiancé instead of my boyfriend, and when Jeremey and I did our dance, our rings would catch in the light and I would remember I was getting married, which always made me feel good.

The other problem I had was one Sally told me was a common problem for engaged couples, which everyone asking when we'd set a date for the wedding ceremony. We had not set a date yet because right now our focus was the vote and too much planning at once would upset Jeremey, so we'd decided to make those decisions later in the summer, since we weren't in a hurry. But it was always the first question people asked, and it was annoying.

I did feel a little more adult, being engaged. Jeremey said the same thing, though he said it wasn't so much grown up as that he belonged.

"It's such a normal thing, to be engaged. Living at The Roosevelt makes me feel like a regular person, no different than anyone else in Ames or the rest of the country. Being engaged for me is similar to you getting a job a Workiva. It's a life step I wasn't sure I was going to get to take. I'm glad I get to do it. It's not why I said yes to you, but it's a nice benefit."

I thought about trying to work something about that into my speeches but it was personal between Jeremey and me. I kept it in mind, though, because it was just another thing The Roosevelt Project and The Roosevelt Foundation stood for: making safe places for people like Jeremey and me, where we could feel normal and do whatever we wanted.

"What normal do you want?" I asked Darren one day when we were sitting together in my apartment. He was visiting me, helping me with a program on my computer. "I have my job and my engagement to Jeremey, my apartment here, and The Roosevelt Project. What are you looking for? Not for other people, but for you?"

Darren considered this before signing to me. *I think I would like to fall in love. With a person in real life, not online.*

I was surprised to hear him say this, because usually Darren didn't want to do this. He said he preferred to keep romantic relationships confined to people on the Internet where they couldn't get complicated with physical expectations. I signed back to him. *Do you have someone you're in love with?*

Darren made his sign for no—he doesn't care to shake his head. *But I think I let myself hide too much when I lived at Icarus. Being with The Roosevelt Blues Brothers has taught me to let myself be with other people. To be myself in my body as well as my mind. I want to find someone who wants to go on walks with me and watch movies with me and play games and get in fights, and care for me. Someone who doesn't care that when I laugh I bark like a dog.*

I smiled. *I like your laugh. It's sharp and pointed.*

Yes, but I can't fall in love with you because you love Jeremey. Also you focus on sex too much.

It was true, I did prioritize sex, and I was in love with Jeremey. *There will be other people who like your laugh. We'll find them.*

Darren used his laugh then, but it was a soft bark. *Are you Super Emmet now, saving everyone? You should save David too. He wants a partner more than me.*

I wanted to help David too, yes, but first I had to figure out how to shelter the sea. *All the Roosevelt Blues Brothers are super. We'll save each other, and everyone else too.*

We kept trying, kept going to our events, kept spreading our message. Darren worked hard online, boosting our videos in chat rooms local, statewide, and beyond. We needed the votes from people in Iowa, but he pointed out it didn't hurt to keep the message coming in from the outside as sometimes pressure worked best from the outside in. David continued to be the resident charmer, always working the front lines of our events and sometimes going with his father to talk with people at private functions for the foundation. Jeremey continued to help each of us in his own way, and though he was the invisible Blues Brother in many ways, he was also the one we relied on the most, because he was always there, propping us up, offering the hand of support we didn't know we needed.

I tried not to be overconfident, but I did feel good about our chances. So did Kaya, and so did Bob.

"The numbers look good," Kaya told me one day after work. "The Roosevelt Foundation is just getting started, but it's strong, and the polls are in our favor. The actual vote among the representatives is still a dead heat, but what I hear is the opposition is running scared. *They* think we're going to win, Emmet."

I was excited about this news, but in the end I think it would have been better if Kaya hadn't told it to me. It made me lower my guard and let me be ruled too much by my emotions, and when RJ King found me, I wasn't ready for him.

It was after an event in the park in Story City. The

other Blues Brothers and I had gone after our performance to enjoy the antique carousel. They turned the calliope off for us while we rode as otherwise it would be too loud. David needed to go to the restroom once we were done riding, so Jeremey went with him to help, and Darren joined them in case they needed more help, and I decided I would make sure Bob and Kaya didn't need anything as they finished talking with donors. They had told us we didn't need to be around, but I thought I would make sure they hadn't changed their minds.

I didn't find Bob or Kaya in the pavilion, but I did find RJ King. When he saw me, he stopped talking to the man he was having a conversation with and came over, wearing a smile I didn't like.

"Mr. Washington. How lovely to see you. I was hoping I would run into you, and here you are. Might I take a few minutes of your time to make you a proposition? Come walk with me outside. It's such a lovely day."

I thought about saying no to him, but I noticed people were watching us, people who might be donors Kaya and Bob needed. My octopus stirred, uncomfortable with RJ King's trick and the situation in general. I decided the best move would be to follow him because I could always get away from him outside, which would also mean other people wouldn't see me leaving.

I followed him out the door, humming softly.

He was right that it was a lovely day. The leaves

were full on the trees now, and a soft, warm wind made them rustle as we walked beneath them. He had a large stride, but he didn't rush me, which was kind of him at least.

"Your project is doing well, Emmet." His voice wasn't loud and slippery as it normally was. It was as if he had taken off a jacket, and this was the real RJ. "I will admit I underestimated you and your friends. I'm impressed. Well done."

I wasn't sure what to say, so I didn't say anything. I thought about getting away from him as I'd originally planned, but since he wasn't being an asshole, I decided I could stay a little longer. Maybe I would discover something that could help us beat him.

He continued to speak, still calm, still unlike the usual RJ King. He was almost kind, in fact. "This being said, as much as I admire what you've been able to do—perhaps because of how much I admire it—I wanted to let you know, there's no way you're going to get what you want. And I suspect I know your answer already, but I wanted to put this on the table all the same. If you were willing to stop now, to quit flaming the fires and ramping people up and making things annoyingly difficult for me, I'd be willing to quietly incorporate some of your ideas into my plans once the bill is passed. Not all, of course. They're too expensive and my investors would never stand for them. But I could work some of them in as a gesture of my appreciation."

I stopped walking and stared at his back, not sure what he was saying.

He stopped too and turned to me. His face hadn't changed, but his tone was flatter now. "It's not an offer I'll repeat. You're making headaches for me, and I'd like to see them go away. But understand me when I tell you, there's no way you'll win. Whatever that woman is telling you, whatever fairy tales you're spinning, at the end of the day, I'll prevail. So if you want any victory at all, Emmet, this is where you take it. Here and now, in this park. You have my word I'll keep my promise. I'll let you tell me what parts you can't live without, and I'll be honest about which ones I can work in. I know what you think of me, but I'm not a monster. I'm a man. A father, a grandfather. I respect you, what you've done. I want to help you. This is how I can do that. Let me, Emmet. Let me help you."

My octopus writhed, but it was more confused than upset. I understood what it was feeling. I had to rock and flap gently as I tried to find a way to respond. "You could help me by helping us win. You could join our foundation. You could back our project. You could get out of our way and help us get votes."

"That wouldn't help my business or the people involved in my business. I have to put them first."

"I have to put my people first. They don't want money, either. They want lives."

"My businesses want to give your people lives. Better ones."

Now I was angry, and so was my octopus. I didn't like the way he said *your people* either. "No you don't, because you don't listen when we tell you the lives you're offering us are bad ones, ones we don't want."

"Life isn't always about what we want."

"Except when you want to give things to the people in your businesses."

His smile was flat and cold. "You're too young to understand the way the world works, but one day you will."

"Bob is the same age as you, and he understands it the same way I do. So does my mother, and Dr. North, and most of the medical profession in the country. You twist facts until they look like the ones you want them to be. You create the definition of normal that suits you best, but there's no normal, RJ King. You can think you're not a monster, but to me and to all the people like me, you're the enemy. No, I won't let you help me. And no, I don't believe it's guaranteed you're going to beat us."

King held up his hands. "Yes, this is what I suspected you would say. But I had to try." He sighed and lowered his hands. "I do wish you well, Emmet. I hope your facility is able to stay solvent despite what I know about its projected trajectory. I hope your marriage to your friend is a happy one, and I hope I'm able to help you find happiness."

I never, ever wanted RJ King to be a part of my happiness. "I don't need you to give me anything, or any of my friends. And we *will* all be happy. We'll beat you too."

RJ King didn't say anything, only shook his head as he turned away from me and walked across the park.

I DIDN'T TELL the others about RJ King's comments to me, not right away. I told Jeremey once we were alone in our apartment that night, lying on my bed with him, as he had his arms around me, being my sensory sack.

Jeremey was upset, but he kept calm as best he could. "He's a terrible man. But you're amazing for being able to keep your cool around him. I would have cried or run away, or maybe hit him."

I hadn't wanted to hit him, or run. But I did hate him more every time I thought about him. "Do you think he was bluffing, or do you think he knows something about the vote? Do you think he's right, that we have no chance of winning?"

Jeremey sighed. "I have no idea. I want to think he's bluffing, but there's no way to tell, and in the end, does it matter? It's not as if we're going to stop. At the end of the day we have to push forward and hope for the best. We're going to get people to the rally, and we're going to get those representatives to vote."

He was right, of course, and so I did my best to put it out of my mind. It wasn't easy, though, and the next day I told the others, first Darren and David and then Kaya and Bob. Darren and David were both angry, especially David, and so were Kaya and Bob. Kaya got one of her funny looks, as if she wanted to throw things, and Bob started touching his face a lot, frowning at the floor. I asked them the same question I'd asked Jeremey. "Do you think he's right? Do you think they will win?"

Kaya shook her head. "Absolutely not. The polls are against them. We still don't know how the representatives will swing, but if their voters are telling them to vote for us, how do you think they will go? I feel good about our chances. Mostly I'm furious this jerk thought he could bully you. Was he trying to rattle you? Make you upset?"

I considered this. "No. He wanted me to know he wasn't a monster."

"*Ah*. Cleaning his conscience. Good for you for not letting him off the hook." Kaya brushed her hands together. "I've never wanted anything more than how much I want to beat this man. Not only to win for our cause but to *defeat this jerk*. I hate his kind. I want to see him go down, and I want you to be the one who does it, Emmet."

I was less interested in taking people down and more concerned about protecting The Roosevelt and our project, but I knew what she meant. It was what Darren had asked me about, the Super Emmet thing. I did want to be a hero. I wanted my Elwood Blues moment.

I only hoped my algorithm could hold, that it

would be enough.

Finally, they set a date for the vote. It would be the last Friday in June, which meant now we knew how much time was left between now and then to get our work done. We scheduled our last events, our final rallies, and we organized a rally for the day of the vote at the statehouse, for people to go and talk to their representatives and to gather on the grounds outside and be seen for the cameras as the vote came in. Hopefully it would also be a victory party afterward.

We had contacts from groups outside of Iowa too, people who wanted to work with the foundation and model their fight on the one we'd begun in Iowa. They were waiting to see how well it worked with the legislature, but even if it didn't, they said they wanted to use the model, and of course we told them yes.

One more big change came in the space between the announcement and the vote, one that was good but I wasn't sure how I felt about it: Kaya got a new job. She gave her notice at Workiva because as of June 30 she'd be working full-time as the director of The Roosevelt Foundation.

"I'll miss working with you so much." She cried as she told me, pressing a wadded-up tissue to her eyes to catch the tears, but most of them ran down her face anyway. "I know I'll still see you because you'll volunteer with the foundation, but it won't be the same as working at Workiva. But I want to help build what we've started, to protect it. I hope you understand."

I did understand, and I thought she'd make a great director. But I would miss her too. I wished she could do both jobs. I tried to tell her all this, but I ended up rocking and hugging her and crying a little too.

I didn't have a lot of time to be sad, though, because we were so busy getting ready for the lobby day. I was helping Darren with some of the online things, and so were Jeremey and David. People from all over the world wanted to know how the vote was going to go. We had become a movie everyone wanted to know the end of.

I just hoped it was a happy ending, not a tragedy.

Two weeks before the vote, I took a walk one night to my parents' house. I had texted them to let them know I was coming over, so my dad was waiting on the front porch for me, hands in his pockets and smiling as I came down the sidewalk. "Good to see you, son."

I signed hello, as I wasn't feeling verbal.

He didn't press me to talk as I went inside, and my mom didn't either once she saw I didn't want to speak. They let me sit in the kitchen and watch them work around me, making coffee and dinner and talking to each other, sometimes to me too but mostly letting me be quiet and by myself.

The house always felt different now, not the same as it had been when I'd grown up in it. I missed it sometimes, though I was glad to have my own place with Jeremey. Sometimes it was comforting to come back and remember what it was like to have this place be my home, to have my mom and dad busy around me when I was overwhelmed. Like right now.

They made me a snack and a cup of herbal tea, and we sat together on the deck, where we could watch trains as they went by. I rocked silently, then started to hum as I got ready to talk. They waited patiently for me to begin, not rushing me.

I'm scared, I signed at last.

My dad put down his cup of coffee. *It's natural to be scared*, he signed.

I felt tears threatening, but I asked the octopus to please keep them back. For once he listened to me.

I don't want to disappoint everyone.

My mom didn't stop her tears, but she didn't look sad. She looked complicated, but if I had to pick an emotion from her face, I would guess proud. *You won't disappoint anyone. We're all so proud of you. No matter what happens, Emmet, we are all so proud of you.*

I couldn't stop my tears anymore either. *I don't want King to win. But I'm afraid he will.*

My dad wasn't crying, but his smile was sad. *If he wins this time, you'll fight and find a way to beat him next time. And we'll help you. So will a lot of people. Remember, Emmet, no matter what it feels like, you aren't facing this alone.*

My octopus stroked my head as the tears fell down my cheeks. *It's going to hurt so much if we lose.*

Now Dad was crying too, one tiny tear that caught

on his nose. *We'll be with you, to help you heal, if that happens.*

We all cried together, for a while. And when I went home, I felt a lot better.

CHAPTER EIGHTEEN

Jeremey

EMMET PRETENDED HE wasn't upset by my parents' reaction to our engagement, but I knew it bothered him. It bothered me too. I supposed I should be glad they weren't overtly fighting us on it, but I was angry they weren't excited for us the way Emmet's family was. I hated how they pursed their lips and looked away, as if we were an embarrassment or something awkward they had to endure. I wanted them to celebrate my happiness, not grin and bear it.

"It makes me so upset." I said this to my sister when I Skyped with her after my meeting with our parents. My original goal had been to tell her about my engagement, but the call quickly became a bitch session, which I felt bad about but couldn't stop. "He makes more money a year than Mom ever did before she retired, and he's smarter than both of them put together. He got me Mai when he saw I needed something more to cope with my daily life, and arranging for her was no small feat. He single-handedly got the ball rolling for The Roosevelt Project, which is now a battle against the state legislature, and people all over the world are in contact with us, with *him*, wanting to know how he did it. *That guy*, Jan, wants to marry me. But all Mom and Dad can see about him is that he has autism, and they don't like it."

She leaned back in the couch she was sitting on, clearly worn out. "Look, you've known our parents are headcases for a long time now. Why you thought they were going to be different over this, I'm not sure."

I stared at the keyboard. "I didn't think they were going to be different. I…don't know. I can't not feel the way you do, is all."

She made a quiet *harrumph* sound, and when I glanced at her face, she was smiling wanly. "I didn't say I didn't feel. I keep telling you. I moved away from them and rarely come home for a reason."

"Yes, but I don't want to move away. And I wish you *were* here. It would be nice to walk down the street to family I actually want to see."

Jan laughed. "I'm not moving home, and even if I did, it absolutely wouldn't be down the street, not anywhere close to them. However, you're right. I need to come home more to see you. I know it's not easy for you to come to me."

"Maybe you can come for Lobby Day. We want to have a big crowd at the capitol."

Jan raised an eyebrow. "*You're* going to be in a big

crowd at the capitol?"

I blushed, but nodded. "Yes. With the rest of the guys, and Mai. I'll be okay because we'll be in our Roosevelt Blues Brothers costumes and we'll be on a stage with a rest area off to the side where I can go if I need a break. We have a permit to organize there and perform. It's a rally. A local drag queen is going to come and pretend to be Shakira while we perform 'Try Everything.' It's going to be fantastic."

Jan smiled. "You've blossomed at The Roosevelt, you know? I'm so proud of you."

"Thanks. Me too." I lifted my chin. "So will you come? Be proud of me in person?"

She laughed. "All right, I'll see what I can do about time off. Text me the date. I'm not promising anything, but I'll do my best."

In the end, she was able to get the time off, several days off in fact, and she booked a hotel in Ames, though Emmet's mom said she could stay at their place if she wanted. Darren's parents were coming too, and they *did* take up Marietta's offer of a place to stay. They came two days before the event to help us with final preparations, and Darren went over often to be with them, though sometimes they came to be at The Roosevelt too.

Emmet spent a great deal of time at his computer, either working on his algorithm programs or on the social networks Darren had set him up with, talking to people to encourage them to come to the rally or to remind them to contact their representatives and ask them to vote against the bill. He was worried, I knew, nervous for the outcome, doing all he could to make sure we won, and I did what I could to help him, but I knew there was only so much help I could give. In the end we had to wait for Lobby Day. We had to wait and see whether or not RJ King's threats had been real. We had to see whether the project and the foundation had done enough.

The other residents of The Roosevelt knew we were working on an important project, though not all of them understood. None of them were coming to the rally with us, and neither Sally nor Tammy was coming down, though they both said they wished they could. Someone was making a live stream, and they promised they'd watch that, but it wouldn't be the same as being there.

It's funny, but sometimes I thought Stuart might have understood more of what was happening than people gave him credit for. He doesn't have any way of communicating the way Darren does, but I'd noticed he kept trying to interact with us, especially Emmet and Darren. Maybe I was making it up, maybe I was projecting. Or maybe I'd gotten good at reading people with autism. Because when I sat with Stuart in the lounge and he screeched and flailed with his strange gestures...sometimes I thought he was telling me something important. All I know is when I told him, "We're going to do our best to win," he made what sounded like a happy screech to me.

The night before the vote, Kaya and Bob took us out to dinner at Aunt Maude's and let us order whatever we wanted. A lot of people recognized us, and we felt like celebrities as we sat at our table. While we waited for our drinks to come, a woman came over to Emmet with tears in her eyes. She had on an apron, but she looked as if she'd come from the kitchen, not the waitstaff. The waitstaff around her held her shoulders and encouraged her to come forward.

"I'm so sorry for interrupting your meal, but I needed to tell you…" She wiped at her eyes, whispering a *thank you* as Kaya handed her a tissue. "Mr. Washington, my son has autism. We've tried a lot of things to get him to communicate with us, but he had a few bad experiences at an old school before we moved here, and then the move made him worse instead of better. Then he saw me watching your video on Facebook, and now he watches you seven or eight times a day, the 'Try Everything' videos and the 'Happy' one. He still isn't talking, but he's singing along with the videos, which is a big step for him, and he sings it all day long and will use it to talk to me sometimes, when he's feeling good. If he sees your picture in the paper or online, he gets excited and lights up. You're his hero, Mr. Washington, but you're mine too." She started crying again, but she kept talking. "You gave me back my baby. Thank you so much. *Thank you so much.*"

She had appeared in the space between Emmet and

me, so Emmet stared at my shoulder as she spoke. When the silence went on too long and she became embarrassed and excused herself, apologizing over and over for interrupting us, Emmet held up a hand, first staying her, then signing to me, with shaking hands.

Please ask her to wait.

Most people at the table wouldn't be able to read Emmet's expression, but between his shaking hands and the way he had begun to rock himself ever so slowly in his seat, I knew he was feeling emotional, that this woman's story had moved him and he needed a moment to compose himself before replying to her. To be honest I was feeling pretty emotional myself, but for Emmet's sake I pulled myself together and addressed the woman.

"He's asking if you would please wait a minute. He needs to collect himself before he can reply to you, but he doesn't want you to leave yet. Thank you for understanding."

The woman blinked at me, glanced at Emmet, then softened before turning to me. "Oh—yes, that's fine. I *am* sorry for butting in, though. I know I shouldn't have, but I couldn't help myself. I work in the kitchen, but I heard from the waitstaff that The Roosevelt Blues Brothers were out here, and I couldn't miss my chance. You've all meant so much to me and my family. I wanted to let you know, especially today, before the vote tomorrow. We won't be able to go to the rally because it would be too much for my son—I'm homeschooling him right now, and he'd love to watch you perform, but he can't handle the stimulation. We go by The Roosevelt on our way home from the grocery store sometimes, though, because I told him it's where Emmet from the video lives. We play the song and he sings along. He gets so happy."

"I'm so glad to hear it." I really was. "You should stop and see us sometime. We have a playground in the back. He could use the swings. A lot of the neighborhood kids do."

"I don't know if he's ready for that, but thank you. I'll remember." She wiped her eyes again. "Anyway, about the rally. We contact our representative every day. She's come to our house and met with us, and I wrote up a statement for her to read on the floor. Our whole family has contacted their representatives, and most of them live in a conservative district. So hopefully it helps."

"What is your son's name?"

Both the woman and I startled at Emmet's voice. "Neil."

"How old is Neil?"

"He's eight."

"Do you have a smartphone with a video camera?"

"I do. Why?"

Emmet lifted his gaze to the centerpiece in the center of the table. "David."

David and the rest of the table had been listening to the whole conversation between the woman and

Emmet and me. "Yeah?"

"I need to borrow your sunglasses."

David reached into the pocket on the side of his tray and pulled out his sunglasses, which were the same as our Blues Brothers sunglasses. He liked the ones we used for our costume so much he'd ordered a second pair for personal use, and he always had them with him. He passed them to Darren, who passed them to me, and I handed them to Emmet.

Emmet slipped them onto his face. "I want you to record something for Neil, please."

"Oh—yes, please, that would be wonderful!" The woman shifted in place, accidentally almost stepping on Mai. I gave a quiet command to Mai to move to my other side as the woman apologized, and I decided I didn't want to think of her as "the woman" any longer.

"I'm Jeremey Samson." I held out my hand. "What's your name?"

"Amanda Beatty. Sorry, I didn't introduce myself properly earlier."

"It's fine." I let go of her hand and nodded to her other hand, where she was pulling her phone out of her purse. "Go ahead and take your video whenever you're ready."

Everyone else was still watching us, Kaya in particular, but no one said anything as Amanda set up her phone and Emmet arranged himself on his chair in what I knew was his best Roosevelt Blues Brothers pose. When Amanda gave him the thumbs-up sign, indicating she'd begun filming, Emmet began to speak.

"Hi, Neil. This is Emmet Washington, one of The Roosevelt Blues Brothers. I'm here with your mom, who says you like to watch our videos. She says you're the same as me, that you have autism." The corner of his mouth lifted in a little Emmet smile, and he rocked in his chair, humming, and I hid my own grin, because I knew he'd done it on purpose, letting himself rock and hum so Neil could see him doing it. "That's cool. It means you're a Roosevelt Blues Brother too. You don't need to have the sunglasses or the hat or the suit to be one, either, though they're fun to have, and you can make your own kind at home. They should be clothes you feel good in, that don't itch or make you feel uncomfortable. So if a suit similar to ours doesn't feel right, don't worry. A real Roosevelt Blues Brother finds their own suit. Also a Roosevelt Blues Brother can be a girl. So if you meet a friend who wants to be a Roosevelt Blues Brother with you and she's a girl, it's okay. You can call it a different name too.

"What matters is you're like me and my friends, Neil. You're special. No matter what anyone at school tells you, no matter what laws anyone passes or doesn't pass, you're a superhero. You have superpowers. You can see and hear things other people can't. Feel things other people can't. Sometimes other people get jealous of your powers and say mean things. Ignore them. You're a Roosevelt Blues Brother. Roosevelt Blues Brothers don't care about that stuff, because we're cool. We're better than those people. We don't let people get us down. We don't quit. If someone tells us no, we find another way.

"I hope I get to meet you someday, Neil. I bet you're a super-cool Roosevelt Blues Brother. I'm going to end this video now and have my dinner, but you take good care of your mom and your family, superhero. Don't forget to try everything, and stay happy." He paused for a second, then added, "That's the end of what I want to say."

Amanda had already stopped the video. She was crying, and so was Kaya, and so was the waitstaff and half our table, to be honest. I was close, but I was so proud of Emmet, so overcome, I couldn't, not quite. Also I knew it would confuse him if I did right then and there, so I held it together, as best I could anyway.

"Thank you." Amanda's voice was a whisper as she put the phone away. She didn't attempt to wipe her tears, but she also looked as if she wanted to hug Emmet, though she made no effort to do so. "Thank you so much, Mr. Washington."

"You're welcome. And you can call me Emmet." Then he turned around in his chair. "Excuse me. I would like you to go now."

The woman apologized and rose, and Kaya quickly followed her, going, I knew, to smooth over Emmet's rough edges. It was funny because you'd think someone who had a son with autism would be accustomed to bluntness, though I also knew from living with both

Darren and Emmet that autism came in many shapes and sizes. I also knew Emmet's bluntness could be tough to take at times no matter how accustomed you were to it.

What I also was aware of, however, was right now the reason Emmet was so curt was he too was overwhelmed. I knew he didn't want to talk, knew he wasn't asking anything from me because he was processing the encounter in his own way. That said, as I rubbed my thumb along my engagement ring, I acknowledged *I* needed a little something from him. Or rather, I needed to tell him something.

Pulling out my own phone, I typed a message on a notepad and set it on the table between us, in the range of his camera vision where I knew he could see it.

I love you.

He didn't react, not at first. But eventually he picked up my phone, held it for a moment, then put it down. When I glanced at it again, it read:

J: I love you.
E: I love you too.

CHAPTER NINETEEN

Emmet

WOKE UP the morning of Lobby Day and stared at my ceiling, certain we would win.

It felt like my algorithm. Part of my brain had been working on the formula this whole time. It had finally discovered the missing parts, and now it knew. I couldn't quite work out how I was so sure, but I wasn't nervous anymore. We were going to get what we needed. The bill wouldn't pass. Everything would be fine.

Everything would be fine.

I hummed to myself as I showered, shaved, and got dressed. Jeremey met me in the hallway as I went to the kitchen. He was still half asleep, but he smiled at me, his hair all messy and his eyes half closed. I stopped him and kissed him though he hadn't brushed his teeth yet.

We're going to win. It's going to be fine.

We were all nervous as we loaded the van. Kaya

kept double-checking things and asking David if his dad had other supplies we'd need. Darren kept looking at his social media sites and rocking in place. Jeremey stroked Mai's head and put his hand on my leg. David was grumpy and picked fights with Kaya. Everyone was on edge. This wasn't going to help us with our performance.

I wanted to give a pep talk like in the movies, but I didn't know any pep talks. I should have thought to memorize one. I looked them up, but the only one that sounded good was the one from *Henry V* or *Independence Day*, and we weren't fighting the French or aliens from space. I thought about the one from *Rocky Balboa*, but it talked too much about hitting people. So in the end I let them be nervous until we passed the Interstate 80 interchange, when I reminded Kaya to put the music on.

We calmed somewhat as we sang the song a few times, and by the time we got to the parking lot we were laughing and teasing each other again. Bob was already there along with the tech people setting up our stage—my mom was there too, and my dad, and Althea, and Jan, and Darren's parents and the rest of David's family. There were all kinds of people there, in fact, and more came every minute. Within an hour of our arrival, the capitol green was full of people, chanting and clapping and dancing to the music coming from the speakers set up on the stage.

We weren't the only people scheduled to perform,

but we were the headliners. While we got into our costumes, local bands played, and Kaya and other members of the foundation spoke to the crowd. We were told the vote would happen in the early afternoon, and the plan was to warm up the crowd and then pack the auditorium and the rotunda and lobby of the building with people to pressure the lawmakers. With this many people, I couldn't see how they could do anything but vote the bill down. There were more people than could fit in the seats in the chamber, than could safely fit in the lobby.

We're going to win, I told my octopus.

Once we were dressed, we stood in the wings of the stage, waiting for our turn. A drag queen was on stage now, the Shakira impersonator who would be performing with us this time. She'd come to rehearse with us a few times this week, and it was fun to work with her. Once we were done, I would give my speech, we'd shake hands at the edge of the rope line, and then we'd move inside.

The rally was the biggest crowd we'd performed for yet, and when we came out, I was nervous at first. My octopus went nuts for a few minutes. But I focused on my brothers, on Jeremey, and it was okay.

It was scary, but it was exciting too. We really were rock stars on that stage. Everyone loved us, and we felt like heroes. I understood then how much we *were* heroes to all those people there. I realized how much good we were about to do, how many people we were about to help by stopping this bill and building The Roosevelt Foundation, and I was proud of myself.

I sang along sometimes instead of lip-syncing—we didn't have microphones, so no one could hear me, but I could feel the song in my chest, and it made me happy. The music buzzed in me, and though it was a little loud, I didn't mind. I spun Jeremey around, felt my octopus flutter at his smile, and in that moment, my life was the most perfect it had ever been.

"Stopping this bill is only the first step," I told the audience during my speech. It was what Kaya and the rest of the foundation board had decided I should say, and I agreed with all the words, feeling them hum in my chest just as the song had. "We need to take serious steps to care for every resident of the state of Iowa, including those with mental health problems and those with special needs. We need to not think about shutting people like me and my friends away but helping us thrive and become contributing members of society. We need to think about how to give everyone quality of life, not simply providing the bare minimum to keep people alive. We need to make ending abuse and neglect a priority. And most of all we need to stop making the first question we ask, 'How much will this cost?' We need to ask instead, 'What does this population need?' and then problem-solve how to fund that need."

Kaya had told me to pause for applause here, and people did clap, so I waited until they were finished before I continued. "Now let's go tell our elected officials what we think they should do on our behalf and not let special interests tell them instead. Our assistants will help you approach the capitol in an orderly fashion, and if you're not able to get inside, don't worry. We have ways for you to still be part of the process. Thank you for coming—today you're all Roosevelt Blues Brothers!"

They cheered at this, and David and Darren and Jeremey raised their hands in the air with me as the audience did the same. I'd noticed there were more than a few people who'd come in Blues Brothers outfits, or a version of the outfit, which was fun. Several people in wheelchairs were dressed up, and when we did the rope line, they came up to David to talk to him. Jeremey and I had to stop to have our picture taken with a girl with Down syndrome, and several other people too. But we couldn't stay long, because we had to go to the capitol—Kaya had gotten word the vote would happen soon.

Someone started singing "Try Everything" as we rounded the corner to the entrance, and the song echoed in the building as we made our way into the rotunda area, where we were told we had to be quiet as we entered. Because of David's chair, Kaya and The Roosevelt Blues Brothers had to be seated on the main floor, so we walked straight on in, right in the same place as the representatives themselves. Bob, my mother, and the others were up in the balcony.

I'd never been in the house chamber. It was old and beautiful and intimidating. The windows were high and had big red curtains. There were tall pillars all around, and everything seemed too fancy. We sat in chairs instead of the rows of benches because of David, and I was glad because the old seats didn't look comfortable.

There were so many people, and so much was going on. I had to rock in my chair, back and forth, and I hummed softly under my breath. Something had changed, somehow, from walking through the rotunda to here. Outside and in the hallway, I'd still felt certain we would win. In here, though, my algorithm felt strained. As if suddenly I had discovered a variable that mattered a great deal, one I hadn't accounted for.

It was almost all men in the room at the desks in a half circle. Older white men who didn't smile, wearing suits and ties, talking to younger people in suits running around and bringing them things. They spoke to each other too, standing off to the side in pairs and in threes, sometimes in small groups. They whispered or spoke in low voices at pitches that made my octopus uneasy. Sometimes they worked on computers, but mostly they spoke to one another, their heads close together. Even if I could have read faces, I think I would have had a difficult time understanding them.

RJ King was there, in the desks, talking to the men in suits.

I drew a breath and flapped twice, my algorithm

shuddering.

Kaya appeared, smiling as she sat beside Jeremey. "They're about to call for the vote. We're holding out for three representatives, but our people are working the floor, and everyone knows about the crowd outside the capitol. They're still singing and chanting. It's all over. There's no way they can vote for it now."

She said this, but my camera eyes tracked RJ King as he wove through the desks, through the men in suits. Smiling. Touching. Talking.

I flapped again.

I wasn't sure we were going to win anymore.

They called for the representatives to vote for the bill, for our bill, the one we wanted them to vote down.

I watched the board on the wall where they displayed the count.

It took several minutes, each side rising in bursts as the representatives pushed their buttons on their desks. Some weren't there, so they didn't push. Some were still talking, so they didn't vote right away.

Some of them were talking to RJ King.

None of us spoke. We all watched the board, waiting to see the final tally. Except I knew how many representatives there were, how many no or yes votes we needed in order to have a winner, so I knew the number we needed to reach to be safe. I kept waiting for it, watching for the number to rise.

All the while I wondered if I should have been on the floor before the vote too. I wondered if I should have been shaking hands and smiling. If I should have been talking in low voices instead of giving speeches in a silly outfit. I watched the YES numbers climb higher and higher, always higher than the NO, and I kept thinking how we had been outside, singing and dancing, while RJ King had been in here, shaking hands with men in suits.

He'd told me he was going to win.

The math was proving he had been correct in his prediction.

I've always liked my camera eyes. I enjoy being able to watch people and see things without people realizing I can see them. But as the final votes came in and the bill officially passed, I didn't care for my camera eyes at all. Because the whole room stared. Everyone looked at me, their faces complicated, as the crowd roared in shock and anger, as the state troopers called for order.

RJ King looked at me too, his face smiling and ugly at the same time. Then he turned away and talked to another man in a suit, his usual RJ King smile back in place.

"Emmet." Jeremey's voice was a whisper. He was upset.

I was too. I could feel my feelings, so many of them at once, coming at me in a great big wave.

The sea I had not been able to shelter.

My hands shook as I signed to Jeremey. *I need to leave right now.*

Jeremey took my hand, helped me to stand. Someone grabbed my other hand—it was Darren. Tears streamed down his face as he called out, a single syllable, sad and broken in the center.

One of my tears fell as we left, Mai leading us and David coming up behind, holding on to Darren's other hand.

CHAPTER TWENTY

Jeremey

I COULDN'T BELIEVE we actually lost.

Part of me was sure it had been a mistake. How could they vote for the bill when so many people had showed up to tell them to vote against it? *How?*

It was as if from the moment the call went out that the bill had passed, that we had lost, the world rippled. I felt like I'd fallen into the wrong timeline. I was *sure* we'd win. I was sure we *had* won. This had to be a mistake. It wasn't possible for us to have lost. Not with all these people. Not with all our chanting and our...

It didn't make sense. How could we have lost? *How?*

As I hurried with the others through the crowd, as Kaya and Mai cleared us a path through the people crying and whispering—*There they go, that's them, The Roosevelt Blues Brothers, the ones who sang, oh my God, they must be so upset right now*—all I could think was how this was a mix-up, how somewhere else there was a version of me celebrating our victory, not rushing away trying not to cry.

Except I *was* crying. Tears kept running down my face, and by the time we left the building, I was sobbing.

The others were too—Darren kept his head bowed, but he would make these little gasps every now and again, and his shoulders would shake. Emmet was flapping, the kind of flapping he did when he didn't want to flap but couldn't help himself. David wept, hard enough he was making it difficult for himself to breathe, and he had to work to keep his airway clear.

Mai kept trying to soothe me, pawing my leg to comfort me, but I didn't know how to explain to her there was nowhere to take me right now, no way to calm me. This was a hurt she wasn't trained to mend, that nothing could fix.

Kaya was crying too, but she kept pulling herself together—she'd sort of fall to pieces, see how lost we were, then straighten up and find some kind of new strength. "I can't get a hold of Bob or Marietta. They were up in the balcony, and there are too many people using cell phones. Signal's jammed." She wiped her eyes furiously, trying to pull herself together. "I'll get the van and bring it over. You guys wait over there by the loading zone, okay?" She left, but she kissed us all on the forehead first, even Darren. "It's going to be okay." Her voice broke, and new tears fell from her eyes. "We're not going to give up, do you hear me?

We're not done fighting. Nothing stops The Roosevelt Blues Brothers. I've got your back. And right now I've got your van."

I felt lost when she left. There were too many other people around us, all of them staring. We were still in our costumes, and for the first time I didn't feel cool in them. I felt conspicuous. We weren't the heroes anymore, or at least not right now. We were the losers. We were crying, vulnerable, falling apart, descending into the aspects of our disabilities we didn't want put on display. I could feel my panic attack ready to burst out of me. Emmet looked as if he wanted a wall to bang his head against. David was jerky and upset, drooling from his crying. I didn't know Darren's breakdowns well enough to predict them, but I knew it wasn't pretty either, that he'd start making noises and gestures that would make him seem strange and awkward, unfamiliar.

A woman came out of the crowd, tears on her face. She had her hands up in front of her in a kind of *Don't mind me, I'm harmless* gesture. "Let us help you. Let us help you get to the loading zone." More tears fell, and her voice broke, but she kept going. "Tell us what you need, and we'll help you."

Darren tugged on my arm and signed desperately. I swallowed the lump in my throat, watching him sign. Then I took deep breaths to calm myself and repeated what he'd said out loud. "We need less people looking at us. We need a safe space."

The woman nodded, but before she could speak, a man appeared beside her. He faced the crowd and cupped his hands around his mouth.

"*Hey.* Everybody, turn to the parking lot, and quiet please. The Roosevelt Blues Brothers need our help."

He had to shout it a few more times, but soon people quieted, and they started to turn away from us.

The man kept talking. "This is what they asked us for. This is what they need from us so they can get to their van and get out of here safely. Please be respectful and give this to them."

Then the man quieted too, and he also kept his back to us.

We went, slowly, to the loading zone. Emmet flapped more now, and hummed, letting out his pain. His hums were his sobs, and they tore me up inside, mingling with Darren's bark-sobs. We were a kind of funeral procession, David leading, occasionally slamming his fist on his tray and swearing, Mai whining at me, confused because she couldn't decide how to help me and none of her attempts were working.

Everyone had their backs to us, but all the people we passed were crying too. They cried harder as we went by, their shoulders shaking, sobs bursting out at odd intervals, mixing with ours. They stayed turned away, though, and it was easier with them not looking. It was a kindness, to be able to melt down without having as much of an audience, though they could still hear us. Though they still knew.

At some point someone began to sing. It was slow, soft, and disorganized, the voices not quite in sync or in the same key, and at first I couldn't understand what they were doing. They were talking, chanting I supposed, but because I had heard it so much from Emmet, I recognized it as the opening monologue to "Everybody Needs Somebody to Love," the song from the *Blues Brothers* movie.

And then the crowd sang the song to us. Softly. Out of tune. Like a lullaby. Telling us they needed someone to love. Telling us they needed us, us, us. When they got to the instrumental section, they hummed it, and they broke out into parts, some people singing as if they were the instruments, others singing the words. All the while they remained turned away.

Everybody needs somebody to love.

I need you.

Emmet didn't sing along, and he didn't dance. It was the first time I'd seen him hear this song and not join in. I don't know if the singing helped us or not, or if it hurt, or if it did nothing. I suppose it meant something to me, that once we were in the van and we were driving in the silence home to Ames, as I sat hugging Mai, letting her lick my tears, I thought of the huge crowd of strangers singing to us, singing our song. Except it wasn't a song we'd ever sung. I wondered why they hadn't sung "Try Everything," or "Happy." I wonder why they sang that one.

Everybody needs somebody to love.

I need you.

We'd had a party planned for after the vote, but we weren't going to it now. We were going home, to The Roosevelt. Jan had texted me, telling me she'd come over, but I asked her to give me time first. I wanted to make sure my friends were okay and to give myself a little time too.

Except it was almost worse once we were home. The staff and residents from The Roosevelt were there, and they were upset too. The staff had been crying. Some of the residents had been too, but some had never understood what was going on in the first place.

Stuart approached me in the lounge. I didn't want to talk to him at first. I didn't have my usual patience for his loud noises and intensity, and I almost told Mai to make him go away. But the song from the parking lot still echoed in my head. All those strangers singing to us. Helping us.

Everybody needs somebody to love.

I need you.

My tears started up again, but I didn't wipe them away, and I didn't turn from Stuart as he shuffled toward me, as he pressed in too close. His expression was tense, upset.

He knew. From overhearing, from listening to the aides whisper, from watching the feed over their shoulders. He wasn't looking in my eyes, but somehow I knew he knew everything about what had happened. My heart skipped several beats, and the room spun a bit as the world reoriented, my perception shifting. That couldn't be right, though. Everyone had always told me Stuart didn't understand what was going on.

Was Stuart…had everyone…all this time, had we…?

Stuart's moan morphed into a sad screech, and then he threw his arms around my neck and began to rock me gently.

I stood there, dazed, shaking, barely able to breathe as Stuart pressed himself heavily against me. Comforting me. He was comforting me. I shut my eyes, let out my breath. Let him comfort me. Let him love me.

"Thank you," I whispered.

He patted my back clumsily and made a mewling noise, kind of like Chewbacca. My heart clenched. *We've been ignoring you.* But when I pulled away, this thought burning in my heart, no doubt on my face, he'd turned away from me, retreating into his usual Stuart-space.

No, I realized. We hadn't been ignoring him. He'd been ignoring us.

Most of us, anyway. Maybe I'd nudge Emmet to reconsider talking to Stuart more the next time he approached him.

Right now, however, Emmet wasn't going to talk to anyone. Everyone else had gone to their rooms. Emmet was upstairs, and when I caught up with him, he was unlocking the door to our apartment. When he saw me, he signed that he loved me, then went to his room and locked his door. I heard his foam hammer, heard him shout, and then silence. I assumed he was in his closet in his sensory sack.

I lay in my bed with Mai. She brought me my anxiety medicine, and I let it dull the painful edges of my sorrow, but I could find nowhere inside me safe to retreat. Only softer dullness. I kept circling back to the feeling of impossibility, that this was all wrong. This wasn't what was supposed to happen. We weren't supposed to be here.

The drug swamped me, flattening me out, and Mai licked my chin, trying to remind me she was there, to comfort me, but I had too much sorrow inside me. I thought of the people we'd met along our journey, the people we hadn't been able to help. Kaya had tried to boost us up on the drive home, reminding us we had more fighting to do, that we still had the foundation, but it felt so hollow.

They could erase it all so easily. We did so much, we brought *so many people*, and the lobbyists simply walked around the room, shook hands, and took our effort away. For some of us, they took our *lives* away. How was this okay? How were we supposed to fight when they could do that?

How am I supposed to feel like a full person when you treat me like this?

Eventually Mai began to whine, worried for me, tugging at me to tell me she wanted me to get up and walk, to connect with someone. I didn't want to, but I thought she might be right, so I texted Jan. She came to get me, and I left a note for Emmet before I let her take Mai and me to her hotel room, where I let her hold me on her bed, and I cried some more.

I cried so much. I don't know if I've ever cried like that in my life.

"Oh, *baby*." Jan held me close and stroked my hair. She was crying too, but she kept trying to soothe me. "I'm so sorry. I don't know what to say, and I hate seeing you like this. It shouldn't have passed. Everyone is so upset. They had to adjourn the session because the people in the balcony wouldn't stop yelling. I think they arrested some people, maybe, but I don't know. People are still at the capitol, chanting, fighting."

But the vote had still passed. Another sob broke out of me, burning my throat. I didn't know how I could keep crying. I felt as if someone had wrung me out, that there couldn't be anything left, but it kept coming. "We worked so *hard*. And it didn't matter. It didn't matter at all."

"Don't say that. *Don't say that.*" She pulled me closer, kissing my forehead, stroking my hair. "It mattered. It mattered to so many people. To me. To the mom at that restaurant. Did you know she posted the video of Emmet on Facebook, and it's gone crazy viral? It's *everywhere*. People are doing response videos to it too. Do you think that's going to stop because of this vote? Do you think the people who shut down the legislative session and camped out at the capitol are going to simply go home and forget this? Do you think *I* am?"

The deepest well of sorrow rose within me, the thing I hadn't said yet, what I was too ashamed to say. To Jan, here alone, I admitted it in the quietest whisper. "I don't know if I can keep going, though. I don't know if I can do this again."

"*Sweetheart.*" She rocked me gently, her tears falling on my hair. "You don't have to do anything, not yet. Not right away. Rest a bit. Let other people fight for a while. Mend your broken heart. Let us handle things while you recover. It's like Emmet said. We're all Roosevelt Blues Brothers now."

She held me until I fell asleep, and I slept for hours, with Mai beside me. When I woke up, Jan brought me a pizza, and we ate together before she took me to The Roosevelt.

Emmet had come out of his sensory sack—his mother had come over and helped soothe him, and she was at our apartment often for the next week, bringing us meals, helping Emmet. At first he didn't go to work and spent most of his time in his room or in his rocking chair watching trains, but eventually he went back to Workiva, because he agreed a schedule was better for him.

He didn't talk much to anyone, only to me and to his mother. He refused to talk about the vote or the foundation, or the project.

David and Darren were a bit better, though Darren was also subdued. He spent a great deal of time on his computer—a *lot* of time on his computer—and he too wouldn't talk about the foundation or the project or anything that had happened. David, however, was another story entirely. When we went on walks together with Mai, he talked about how he felt, and sometimes he became so emotional he cried.

"I don't understand. It shouldn't have happened. I don't get how they're allowed to just *do that.*"

I didn't understand either. "Kaya says they're counting on people not caring by the time the elections come around. People are too distracted."

"Well, we have to make sure they're not too distracted, then."

I twitched, a flicker of panic rising at the idea of fighting once more only to taste another kind of defeat. I didn't want to do that ever again. But I didn't say so to David.

It was true, though, how other people were still fighting. I could see it. The Roosevelt Foundation was getting stronger every day, and Kaya was clearly thriving, working there. She came by The Roosevelt all the time, and by the second week in July she'd hired David and Darren officially, no longer part of any grant or special project, though they wouldn't be making much money.

She tried to hire me, but I told her I wasn't ready. She said as soon as I was, I had a job waiting for me. I knew, though, I would only ever work as David's aide, never as an official employee like David or Darren. It wasn't the way I was ever going to help shelter the sea.

I did watch Darren and David work plenty, though. Darren's job was to scour the Internet for stories relevant to the foundation and the cause in general, and he was excellent at it. David helped too, but he did more of the sorting, deciding where they went and what they might mean, and talking with people in social situations. In a way I suppose I *was* working for the foundation because I was right there, watching them, helping David when his software couldn't quite do what he needed it to do and I had to give him an assist, helping him set up his appointments with people.

In doing so, I saw not only were other people helping and fighting, I saw how we, The Roosevelt Blues Brothers, had a more significant impact than I had ever imagined.

Jan had told me about Emmet's video going viral, about people doing responses to it, but I didn't understand what she meant until I saw the phenomenon for myself. The original video had hundreds of thousands of hits on Facebook, but many of the responses had high counts too. Some were kids in Roosevelt Blues Brothers outfits, and some were adults or young adults. Some were clearly people like us, people with some kind of disability, but some were people on the mean, and those people usually told stories about family members or friends.

They moved me so much, because they talked about people with social anxiety like me, and they talked about *me*, how the stories about me had helped them feel normal. Some of them talked about David. Some of them talked about Darren—there were several videos of people with cerebral palsy or severe autism with additional complications or a disability that made it difficult for them to speak or made it so they couldn't at all, and Darren was their hero of choice.

But there were *so many* who loved Emmet. So many little boys who said Emmet was their Elwood Blues, their Roosevelt Blues Brother. They sang "Try Everything" or "Happy" or simply stood there flapping and grinning, their gazes locked slightly away from the camera. I wanted more than anything for Emmet to come downstairs to David's room and see them, or to log on to his own computer and see them himself.

Emmet wouldn't.

He got angry if anyone brought up the topic, even three weeks after the vote. He was fine at work, and he didn't have any explosions at The Roosevelt, but this was only if we didn't push him and only if we didn't bring up the vote or anything related to it. Which became a problem as the viral videos kept spreading.

The movement hadn't died. If anything, it had grown, and exponentially. The Roosevelt Foundation had donations pouring in every day from all over the world. The legislators at the statehouse were still inundated with calls, and the governor was under pressure to not sign the bill. The conventional wisdom was he still would, that the vote would pass no matter what, but it felt as if the whole state was on fire. The newspapers were full of angry letters, and the reporters were writing article after article.

And they kept coming to talk to *us.*

Not only local news, either—because of the videos, the national news wanted to talk to us too. The morning talk shows kept playing the video, and they wanted to interview Amanda Beatty and her son, but she hadn't come forward because she wouldn't do it without Emmet. And Emmet wouldn't let us tell him what was going on.

Sometimes I wondered if he knew. He was on his computer, he went to work—he had to have seen or heard some of it. I hated that he wasn't telling me, how he wouldn't let me in. I understood why, but I didn't like it. I didn't care for it at all.

Especially since the more I watched the movement rise, the more I wanted to rejoin it, to take my place inside it again. But I didn't want to do it without Emmet beside me.

The longer our silence went on, the more The Roosevelt Blues Brothers didn't appear, the more the fervor for us rose. Reporters began showing up outside the building. They tried to talk to Emmet on his way to work. They haunted Amanda and her son as they went to the grocery store. They followed David and Darren and me and Mai, and eventually we couldn't go anywhere without being harassed.

I didn't know what to do. I didn't want to argue

with Emmet, because he'd get angry with me. We had to do something, though, and we had to do it soon.

When I had the idea, I wasn't sure if it was a good one or not. I called Kaya, apologizing before I told her because I was already unsure, but she said it was a great idea and wanted to try it right away. So I paced the lounge, making Mai uneasy because she could read my anxiety, but there wasn't much else to do but wait.

When Kaya texted me, *I've got them, we're on our way, get him ready*, I was even more nervous. But I went upstairs, rubbed Mai's head to calm myself, and went into my apartment to talk to my fiancé.

Emmet was in his rocking chair, rocking and flapping his hands. He didn't face me as I came in, but he stopped rocking. "Hello, Jeremey."

"Hi, Emmet." I stood near him, trembling with nerves. "We have a visitor coming to see us. Or, to be accurate, you do. Someone is coming to see you."

He flapped a little harder. "I don't want to see anyone right now."

"It's Neil Beatty."

Emmet stopped flapping. He turned toward me, looking near my shoulder. "He's the boy I made a video for."

"Yes. The reporters are bothering him and his family too. His mother is hoping you'd be willing to meet with him, hoping seeing you will help calm him. She posted the video on Facebook to share with her family, and it went viral." It dawned on me he was letting me talk to him, and everything began to spill out. I tried to keep it from veering into something that would make him shut down, but I felt like I was driving a mine cart on a rickety track with no brakes. "Very viral. A lot of people made response videos, and they're viral too. All the news places want to talk to him, and to you and to us, and it's difficult to make them stop. She isn't sending him to ask you to do anything about that, but if you would talk with Neil, she'd be so grateful." I drew a breath. "We all would."

I didn't know what to expect. I didn't know what he would say, to be honest. All I knew was the whole world balanced on his answer, *my* whole world. *Please,* I begged him silently, knowing he couldn't read the desperation on my face, my hopes, my silent signals. I had to rely on my words, on my logic. On my love, on his.

Please, Emmet. Please come out of your shell again for me. For you. For Neil. For us.

Emmet turned away, rocking and flapping gently, more soothingly. "All right."

I let out the breath I'd been holding. I wanted to hug him so badly, but I knew better, so I hugged Mai instead. "*Thank you,*" I whispered, then hurried to go meet Amanda and Neil.

CHAPTER TWENTY-ONE

Emmet

NEIL BEATTY WAS like me.

His hair was different and his face had a different shape, and it was rounder than mine had been when I was younger. But he was like me, the way I had been when I was his age and still was. I could see myself in the way he moved. The way he averted his eyes, the way his hands wanted to flap. The way his legs didn't want to do what he wanted.

There were other ways too.

He stood near his mother, not touching her, but staying near her space too as he rocked and flapped. Then he hummed and jerked his head. "'Try everything, oh, oh, oh, oh, oh.'" He pointed to his suit, his hat, the sunglasses he was waving in his hands.

Echolalia. His mother had told me he'd been using the song to speak. I didn't need to use the song to speak back to him, though. He'd understand me just fine. But it made me feel warm inside that he was using my song to parrot.

"I like your suit. It's the same as mine." It hurt to say that, though I did like his suit, that he'd had one made to match my Roosevelt Blues Brothers one. The problem was I still didn't want to talk about the project or the vote. Although it didn't hurt as much when I watched Neil. He looked good in his suit.

"He wears it every day." Amanda's voice was a whisper above her son. "I tried to get a second one, but he'll only wear this one, his one Roosevelt Blues Brothers outfit. I don't know what I'm going to do when it wears out."

That made me smile. "I had a cup I had to drink out of. When it got lost, my mom replaced it with one that seemed the same, but I knew it wasn't the right one, and I was sad. But eventually I learned to like the new one too."

Neil kept looking at me—not right at me, but I wasn't looking directly at him either. I noticed everything about him, though. He was fascinated with me, as much as I was with him. I wondered if this was how I had been when I dressed up with my dad to be a Blues Brother. If this is how I would have been if I could have met Dan Aykroyd.

Neil flapped his hands as if he was trying to speak. "'I won't give up, no I won't give in.'"

I wasn't sure what he was trying to say to me through his echolalia, so I waited, but he didn't clarify. It occurred to me he might mean precisely what he said, and then I flapped, gently.

He wound up again. "'I'll keep on making those new mistakes.'" Then he stepped forward and did my dance routine from our performance.

He did it perfectly. He did the whole routine, singing the whole song from that point, doing his best to mimic dancing with Jeremey when it came to the part where Jeremey should have been there.

When the song was done, he flapped and rocked, staring as near my face as he could bear to.

I knew what he was telling me now, and I didn't want to hear it. But I couldn't be angry with him the way I was angry with everyone else. I couldn't walk away from him. It wasn't because he looked like me when I was little either, or because he was a kid.

It was because I knew he was right.

I ignored his mother, forgot the rest of the world. Everyone else had tried to talk to me about this, from Dr. North to my mother to Kaya to Jeremey, but I decided it had to be Neil I confessed this to, that he was the only one who could understand.

"Neil, I couldn't save them. I let everyone down. I wasn't the hero after all. I wasn't Elwood Blues. I let the bad guy win, and it made me sad. I don't want to fight him again."

Neil shook his head vigorously. "'*Try Everything.*'" He pulled a piece of paper out of the pocket of his jacket that was folded up tight, and unfolded it with clumsy hands before pressing it into mine. "'I won't give up, I won't give in!"'

I looked at the paper, reading it as Amanda asked Neil what he'd given me. Neil shooed her away, and I ignored them both. It was an email to Neil, from the *Ellen* show. Inviting him to come. With his mom, and with me, and with the rest of The Roosevelt Blues Brothers.

I shifted my gaze toward Neil, but I already knew what he was going to say.

"'Try Everything.'"

I thought about the reporters bothering me every time I went anywhere. I thought about Jeremey and Kaya and David and Darren, working hard, rejoining the fight. I thought about RJ King, smiling and shaking hands with men in suits, taking the funding for the mental health projects and trying to ruin The Roosevelt and all the projects like it before they had a chance to get started.

I thought about Neil in his Blues Brothers suit, his face as cool and blank as mine and yet full of expression and hope, if you knew how to read it.

I did.

"I want to try everything," I told him.

And the clouds inside me parted as the smile spread across Neil's face.

WE FLEW TO California instead of taking a train.

I investigated Amtrak, because we could have gotten a sleeping car, but the show wanted us to come right away, and they pointed out it would take several days with a lot of switching to get to them by train. Plus the lines were known for their delays. Also Neil hadn't been on a train, and we didn't know how well he'd do on that long of a trip, plus it was tough for David because he had to be on the lower floor, and it was impossible to navigate anywhere else, which made a long trip boring.

So we went by plane. The show paid for our flights, and they booked us first class. This meant we went through different security too, which helped because security is stressful. But Kaya went ahead and talked to them, and it turned out we had fans in the security line. They really liked how Neil had on his Roosevelt Blues Brothers outfit, but when they engaged with him too much, I told them to give him space. I appreciated how they listened right away. Jeremey didn't have any trouble with Mai either, which was good.

I wondered if this meant our message was getting across, that maybe people were paying attention after all. Maybe we hadn't lost.

The flight wasn't direct, so we had a layover in Denver, and we had fans there too. People recognized us everywhere we went. David kept having to lend me his sunglasses so I could pose for pictures with Neil. Eventually Kaya had to ask the airport staff to find us somewhere to sit where we could get away from the crowd, and they put us in a VIP lounge for our airline, and we had free drinks and snacks.

I noticed Neil ate and drank whatever I did, waiting to see what I chose and then taking the same thing. He always sat beside me, and if I ever flapped my hands to relieve tension, he flapped with me, smiling like we shared a secret.

There had been a weird moment at The Roosevelt before we left, with Neil and Stuart and me. We'd been waiting in the lounge to leave, and Stuart came up, I thought to bother me. But he went to Neil instead, and the thing was he didn't bother Neil. Neil seemed happy to see him. It was almost as if they understood each other. On the way to the van that would take us to the airport, Jeremey told me I needed to reconsider Stuart, that lately he'd started to wonder if maybe Stuart wasn't more like Darren than we'd known. Maybe not a Blues Brother, but he was still who we were fighting for, yes?

I told Jeremey I didn't want to think about that right now. But the thing was, every time I looked at Neil, I thought about Stuart.

By the time we landed in Los Angeles I was doing a lot of flapping and humming, and so was Neil, and Darren, and the non-autistic people were doing their own versions of the same, because they were tired and overstimulated too. I worried maybe people here would recognize us the way they had in Denver, and I didn't want to take any photos, but this time there was someone ready to pick us up as soon as we came out of the gate. The escort took us away in a big, black car with tinted windows. He and the driver talked to us through the window of the front seat of the car, telling us we could help ourselves to the refreshments, and there were all kinds of them—little sandwiches, drinks, even hamburgers and cheeseburgers in a heated bin.

The sandwiches were too complicated, too fancy, but they didn't have sauce on them, which was good, because I was able to take them apart and make them simpler with only ham and cheese and lettuce. Neil tried to copy me, but I could tell he didn't care for his sandwich and was nervous. He kept repeating *try everything* in a worried tone.

I turned to Amanda. "What does he normally eat on his sandwiches?"

"Only peanut butter. I should have put some in my carry-on, but I worried they wouldn't let me take it through security."

"Does he like cheese?"

"Some kinds, yes."

I pulled the cheese from my sandwich and broke it in half and passed some to Neil. "Try everything?"

He took it hesitantly, then put it in his mouth. He chewed and nodded. "Try everything."

We ended up eating our sandwich in pieces, the cheese and the bread only, and everyone except for Darren ate cheeseburgers and hamburgers so we could pick apart the sandwiches. I wanted to eat the ham, but Neil had tried it and didn't like it, and if I ate it, he would try too, and this would cause a problem.

I wanted the ham, but I wanted Neil to be calm more.

Once we were at the hotel, Neil went with his mom to his room and Jeremey and I went to ours. It was quite nice and spacious. We had a beautiful view of the city, and I stood at the window with Jeremey, holding his hand, looking at the buildings, the people. But we couldn't see the ocean. I wished we could.

"We'll have some time after the taping." Jeremey squeezed my hand. "We should go to the beach. I've never seen the ocean up close."

I hadn't either. I was glad I would see it for the first time with Jeremey. But then a great feeling hit me, and I checked the clock on the bedstand. The taping wasn't until tomorrow. We didn't have anything scheduled for tonight. "Let's go right now."

"Right now? But I don't think we're close to the shore. And it's late, and everyone is tired. We can't get a ride from anyone."

"It's only seven."

"It's nine for our bodies, which are still on Iowa time. Besides, I think Kaya is about to come ask us what takeout we want to order."

I couldn't get the thought of going to the ocean out of my mind, though, and the idea that no one else would be with us only made the concept better. "We're adults. We can go on our own. We'll take a cab and go ourselves." I tugged on his hand. "Come on."

We immediately ran into trouble with my plan. It

turned out Jeremey was right. We were nowhere near the ocean. Also, cabs were expensive, and I didn't have a comprehensive understanding of L.A. traffic. "You need to wait until after the taping," Kaya insisted. "I promise we'll go, as long as you want to stay, but it has to be after the taping."

I knew I was being unreasonable, but it was as if my octopus had finally realized its natural habitat was close by. Part of me hoped it would hop off and swim away. "Kaya, *I need to go.*"

In the end, we compromised. Kaya called friends of hers who came to get us and take us to the Santa Monica State Beach. This meant we had to wait forty minutes for them to arrive, but it did mean we got to see the ocean that night, and while we waited we freshened up and had something to eat from the hotel restaurant that wasn't picked-apart sandwiches.

Kaya's friends were nice. Stephen and Kari said hello to Kaya, gave her a hug, shook our hands, then took us to the beach. They were friendly but not intrusive, and they let Jeremey do most of the conversation. Mai sat between us, and Kari asked a lot about Mai. They had two dogs, and they loved dogs in general. She didn't try to pet Mai, though, and she didn't talk to Mai, only to Jeremey.

I talked to them a little. They asked me about my work, and I was okay to talk about that. Stephen worked in finance and was interested in the technical details of my job, and I enjoyed sharing them with him.

He was also an author and wrote horror books. I downloaded several so I could read them on the way home. He also liked to play video games. I told him he needed to meet Darren.

We didn't talk about The Roosevelt Project, but I could tell they wanted to.

When we got to the beach, I couldn't quite see the ocean. I could glimpse part of it—the big body of water in the distance, and it was beautiful, but I couldn't view it properly. I was able to see some kind of light display with a Ferris wheel and everything, which Kari said was the Santa Monica Pier. She told us we should go see it, but it didn't have an ocean on it, so I wasn't interested.

There was nowhere to park, so Kari and Stephen found us as quiet of a place as possible, dropped us off, and told us that we should text them when we wanted to go back.

"We don't live far from here. So let us know when you're ready, and we'll be your taxi to Burbank." Kari smiled at us. "Stay as long as you want. It's a great night to enjoy the ocean."

There was noise everywhere, so many people, so many lights and cars, things banging and snapping and popping, but behind all of it there was that sound, something I had never experienced before in real life, only in movies and on CDs. The soft roar and rush of water, crashing and pulling onto sand. Over and over and over.

The ocean.

I heard it before I saw it, as Jeremey took my hand and drew me forward, down the walkway toward the great expanse of sand, until the people and the buildings parted and I could see it.

There it was. The ocean was there, in front of me.

It was so big. I'd known it would be big, but it was *so big*. I tried to calculate how large it was compared to the land mass, but my brain couldn't do it because it was too busy noticing how huge the water was. I hummed at it, flapping my free hand as the ocean sent another wave onto the sand, reaching farther than it had the time before. It was alive. It was a real thing, the ocean. I felt it the way I always felt objects, felt their feelings, attached to it the way Neil attached to that particular suit he wore and I had attached to that one cup when I was young. Autistic people felt differently. We saw the world differently.

I saw this ocean differently.

The ocean was a real thing, and I had love for it. I loved it so much, so quickly it hurt my chest and made me sway, made my octopus quiver with all the emotions inside me. I could watch it reach for the land for hours. For days. It would make me so happy to do nothing but watch this ocean forever.

It was almost better than a train.

It was, actually, better than a train.

Jeremey seemed to think so too. "It's so beautiful." His voice was soft, and he kept squeezing my hand.

Mai wagged her tail as she watched the water come in.

I couldn't use my words yet. I could only watch the water. I could still see the pier in the distance, and there was a great deal of stimulation all around, but the ocean was so big and powerful it overwhelmed everything else. It shut down the other noises for me and made me calm.

We stood there for a long time, until eventually Jeremey spoke again. "Let's take off our shoes and walk in it."

We used one of the bags Jeremey kept in Mai's jacket for catching her dog poop to hold our shoes. I carried them while we held hands and walked in the shallow waves of the ocean. Mai played in the water when Jeremey told her she could. I got wet to my knees, and it was great. My feet were sandy, and I knew I wouldn't be happy when this was done and I had gritty, dirty feet, but the water felt too wonderful. I was walking in the ocean. It was tickling my feet, and Jeremey's feet, saying hello to us. I kept laughing, flapping the hand holding the bag of shoes, almost dropping it, I was so happy. I didn't care anymore that I had flown so far and was overtired. I wasn't tired, not anymore.

I loved the ocean so much.

We stayed until it was dark, until the moon rose above us in the sky and shone down on us, glowing faintly because there were so many lights it had to fight against, but I could see it there, could feel it smiling at us. I flapped at it and whispered to Jeremey so he could see it too.

"I see Tycho." Jeremey pointed at the moon. His face glowed in the lights from the pier, from the moonlight too. "I wonder if there's moondust rising from it right now, falling slowly in space."

I told him no question, absolutely there was.

It was almost eleven when Kaya buzzed Jeremey's phone telling him we really needed to get back. Jeremey texted Kari and Stephen, and while we waited for them to come, we cleaned our feet at an area near the parking lot with sprays just for this purpose. I thought that was clever.

When I finished putting my shoes on and stood, Jeremey was waiting there, looking at me with a serious expression.

"Emmet, I want to get married to you at the ocean. At *this* ocean."

I smiled at him, my heart swelling with warm feelings. "Yes. I would like that too."

Jeremey leaned on my shoulder all the way to Burbank, and I thought about getting married to him as we drove through the darkness. I could still feel the ocean on my feet, on my legs, and as we went to bed, after I made love to Jeremey and lay beside him staring at the ceiling while I waited for him to fall asleep, I felt as if the ocean were moving across my heart too. It felt good. It felt as if it were washing me, and I let it keep coming, because every wave made me feel lighter, stronger.

Then it was morning, and it was time to go to the taping.

Darren had done some research on what would happen at the show, but it turns out he had been wrong. They didn't behave as they usually did for shows. The producer came to our greenroom first thing and asked us what would be the best way to approach the taping to make sure everyone was comfortable, to make sure Neil didn't get over-whelmed, to make sure none of us did either.

I was impressed by that.

Amanda talked with the producer, but I could tell she was intimidated because this was Hollywood, so I talked to Kaya and we basically stepped in and took over. I pointed out Neil would be okay with whatever I did, he'd be okay if I was there, but a big audience might be a problem. I asked if there would be a way to hide the audience from us while Ellen interviewed us, or to let Neil do a test first to see if that many people would be scary.

"You might want to have a plan A and a plan B," Kaya pointed out. "And a plan C might not be a bad idea either."

The producers were okay with this, and later we learned they had plans D and E as well. But Neil was okay with being on stage with Ellen and me, so long as no one clapped and the lights weren't too bright.

Ellen was nice. I liked her face and her smile. She

was patient with Neil, and when she found out he only answered questions with lyrics to "Try Everything" but that Amanda and I could translate them, she acted as though this was an awesome skill he had.

She treated it like a superpower.

She asked me questions too, and of course she asked me about The Roosevelt Project. It was the first time I'd spoken about it since talking with Neil, though I had let Kaya coach me on answers I should give since I was representing the foundation. Except here on the stage with Ellen, with Neil beside me, with the ocean still washing over my heart, I ended up saying different things.

"It was difficult to lose the vote." I rocked in place as I told her this, and I couldn't help flapping my hands. Neil flapped with me, an echo. "We had worked so hard. It made me sad to know we could put so much work into trying to change things and find out we couldn't change anything."

This time when Ellen smiled at me I couldn't figure out what her smile meant. It was tricky. "Well, Emmet, it's funny you should bring that up. I have something I want to show you. In fact, it's something several people want to show you, including your friends and family. I don't know if you've heard, but there's a great deal of video on the Internet about you. Many, *many* people have made videos for you. And that's part of why you're here today, because we wanted to show you those videos, and we here at the show have done a little something extra with them. Will you let me show you something right now? Here on the show?"

"'*Try everything,*'" Neil whispered, flapping enthusiastically.

I nodded. "Yes. I'll watch it."

And on the screen between us, on the wall behind us, a video began to play.

It was the one of me, the one I made for Neil in the restaurant. Or, it was at first. The audio stayed, but there was also a pop song underneath it, something about the future looking good. The video also changed, to one of Neil, and then to another boy, and another.

And another. And another. And another. And another.

There were girls too, and older boys and girls, and adults, and groups of people. Then there were large groups of people. There were famous people, and sometimes people who spoke in foreign languages. The clips went by fast, and sometimes they were only pictures.

Everyone was always dressed up in a Roosevelt Blues Brothers suit. Everyone had a sign that read, "I am a Roosevelt Blues Brother."

Sometimes, if it was a video, not a still, the people said it too. "I am a Roosevelt Blues Brother." Some of the girls said, "I am a Roosevelt Blues Sister," but most of them said Brother even if they were female. It kept going and going, and the song had to be on some kind of loop, because it was an exceptionally long video.

The video changed. It still had people dressed up as Roosevelt Blues Brothers, but now there were words at the bottom. I realized they were tallies. Tallies of money people had raised for The Roosevelt Foundation, or for foundations like ours. It was a lot of money. Whenever famous people came on screen and said they were Roosevelt Blues Brothers, there was a tally too. It always went to our foundation.

Dan Aykroyd was one of the famous people, and he winked at me. "Good job, Emmet. I'm proud to be a Roosevelt Blues Brother too."

I hummed and flapped hard.

The video kept going, and going, and going. It had gone on for at least ten minutes, I realized. More, maybe. They wouldn't ever be able to have that much go into the show.

This meant they had shown this long version just for me.

When it was done, I turned to Ellen, who was looking at me with another tricky smile, and tears in her eyes. "I think you changed quite a bit, Emmet Washington."

I let the ocean wash away the last bit of sadness on my heart. "I think you might be right."

The audience started to clap, forgetting they weren't supposed to, but Neil was okay. He'd done well, and I think he wanted to watch our performance, which was the next part of the show.

But Ellen wasn't done with surprises for us.

She gave us a big cardboard check donation of her own, but then she said she'd heard Jeremey and I were getting married, and she gave us matching fancy tuxedoes and a gift package to get married on the beach in Santa Monica. She told us there was no rush, we could get married anytime we were ready, but she hoped we'd send her an invitation if we had a spare one.

I don't know how she found out about it, since we only decided we wanted to get married there the night before, and we hadn't told anyone. I was starting to think Ellen was magic.

She had one more surprise, though. When Darren and David came onstage to join us, we had already known Ellen would get in a Blues Brothers suit and dance with us too, and we had a space for her in our routine, but she stopped us and said we had to make room for one more person too. We were confused, and then who do you think came onto the stage?

Shakira, the one who actually sings "Try Everything."

So that's how we ended up on the *Ellen* show, dancing with Ellen while Shakira sang for us. While Neil danced in the audience until I motioned for him to come forward and dance beside me on the stage. And as he smiled up at me, big and awkward and beautiful, I realized this was what it would have been like for me if Dan Aykroyd would have invited me up to dance with him when I was little.

Our routine was a bit off while we performed, but they were all new mistakes, so it was okay.

I sang with Shakira a couple of times on the chorus. She smiled at me as we danced together, as I did my Elwood Blues moves with her. Ellen was good too, doing her silly Ellen dance with me, with Darren, with David, with Jeremey, even for a while with Neil until he got overwhelmed and had to go sit with Amanda again.

The best, though, was when I danced with Jeremey. When I spun him in my arms, when the world went away and it was only the two of us inside the space. There were lights and cameras on us, and once this show aired, more people would recognize us in airports. We were going to be celebrities like Ellen.

We were going to keep fighting. We'd keep falling down, and sometimes it would hurt a lot. But I reminded myself Jeremey would always be here with me, inside this dance and outside of it. So would Darren and David and everyone else, even Ellen. Everyone in the video she'd played for me.

I'd had it wrong all along. I didn't have to shelter the sea. I had to find the way to let the sea shelter me. And as the audience's roar washed over me in a wave, as I let the video and everything we'd accomplished sink into my heart, I acknowledged my sea was quite wonderful indeed.

About the Author

Heidi Cullinan has always enjoyed a good love story, provided it has a happy ending. Proud to be from the first Midwestern state with full marriage equality, Heidi is a vocal advocate for LGBT rights. She writes positive-outcome romances for LGBT characters struggling against insurmountable odds because she believes there's no such thing as too much happy ever after. When Heidi isn't writing, she enjoys cooking, reading, playing with her cats, and watching anime, with or without her family. Find out more about Heidi at heidicullinan.com.

Did you enjoy this book?

If you did, please consider leaving a review online or recommending it to a friend. There's absolutely nothing that helps an author more than a reader's enthusiasm. Your word of mouth is greatly appreciated and helps me sell more books, which helps me write more books.

MORE BOOKS IN THE ROOSEVELT SERIES

Book One: Carry the Ocean

Jeremey doesn't judge Emmet for his autism. He's too busy judging himself, as are his parents, who don't believe in clinical depression. When his illness reaches a breaking point, Emmet rescues him and brings him to The Roosevelt, a quirky assisted living facility. As Jeremey settles in, Emmet slowly begins to believe he can be loved for the man he is inside. But before he can trust enough to fall head over heels, he must trust his own conviction that friendship is a healing force, and love can overcome any obstacle.

Book Three: Unleash the Earth (David's story) – OR – Shatter the Sky (Darren's story) 2018
(not sure which is first yet)

Other books by Heidi Cullinan

There's a lot happening with my books right now! Sign up for my **release-announcement-only newsletter** on my website to be sure you don't miss a single release or re-release.

www.heidicullinan.com/newssignup

Want the inside scoop on upcoming releases, automatic delivery of all my titles in your preferred format, with option for signed paperbacks shipped worldwide? Consider joining my Patreon. You can learn more about it on my website.

LOVE LESSONS SERIES
Love Lessons (also available in German)
Frozen Heart (coming soon)
Fever Pitch (also available in German)
Lonely Hearts (also available in German)
Short Stay
Rebel Heart (coming July 2017)

THE DANCING SERIES
Dance With Me (Ed and Laurie)
also available in French, Italian coming soon
Enjoy the Dance (Tomás and Spenser)
Burn the Floor (coming soon)

MINNESOTA CHRISTMAS SERIES
Let It Snow

Sleigh Ride

Winter Wonderland

Santa Baby

More adventures in Logan, Minnesota, coming soon…

CLOCKWORK LOVE SERIES
Clockwork Heart

Clockwork Pirate (coming soon)

Clockwork Princess (coming soon)

SPECIAL DELIVERY SERIES
Special Delivery (also available in German)

Hooch and Cake (coming soon)

Double Blind (also available in German)

The Twelve Days of Randy (coming soon)

Tough Love

TUCKER SPRINGS SERIES
Second Hand (written with Marie Sexton) (available in French)

Dirty Laundry (available in French)

(more titles in this series by other authors)

SINGLE TITLES
Antisocial (coming August 2017)

Nowhere Ranch (available in Italian)

Family Man (written with Marie Sexton)

A Private Gentleman

The Devil Will Do

Hero

Miles and the Magic Flute

NONFICTION

Your A Game: Winning Promo for Genre Fiction
(written with Damon Suede)

Many titles are also available in audio and more are in production. Check the listings wherever you purchase audiobooks to see which titles are available.

CPSIA information can be obtained
at www.ICGtesting.com
Printed in the USA
LVOW08s1036240417
531970LV00001B/66/P